...S COTTAGE
A GHOST STORY

CHARLOTTE WEBB

NENE PUBLISHING

CHAPTER

ONE

"Well, boys," Peter gave each of the dogs a solid rub behind the ears before straightening, "what do you say we beat the sun this morning so we can get in a walk by the river before work?"

With any luck, he'd be able to steal a kiss from Sally while they were in the village, too. She was an early riser just like him. Pretty, too. Nearly as pretty as the sunrise promised to be with her flame-red hair and bright blue eyes. By Peter's reckoning, the only thing his girl lacked was his love of nature. There would never be a quiet evening spent fishing or a hike through the woods with his Sally. She had an aversion for dirt just as strong as his love for it. Still, if he were to someday marry her, she would make the cozy cottage he lived in on the estate into a home. And if her kisses were any hint of what lay beyond them, he might be content to confine his need for nature to working hours. That was something to consider.

"Just not today," he flashed a grin at the Labradors. "We like our bachelor ways too much, don't we boys?"

Peter took the cap and vest that passed as his gamekeeper's uniform from their hook by the door and grabbed the ball, his dogs loved splashing after in the river. He checked his pockets to make sure he had everything before slinging his rifle over his shoulder on the off chance some predator lurked out in the darkness. Foxes were an ever-present problem with the pheasants, and he wasn't about to let one spoil his employer's upcoming plans with an early morning raid on the pens.

Sally would hand him his breakfast from her dainty fingers when he got to the village bakery. She would even have something for Duke and Squire although she was still squeamish around them. There would be a few minutes for some sweet words before they parted ways, too. Maybe this time he could convince her to take a few steps into his world when they shared their next afternoon outing.

Going out with her friends was alright, he supposed. He just couldn't help longing for some time alone with her surrounded by the beauty of the land he spent his time caring for. He wanted nothing more than to run his fingers through his girl's hair while the setting sun danced over it. Maybe even lay beside her on a blanket in the field and point out the constellations overhead with her soft hand in his. Then, he could walk her home under the bright moon and kiss her at the door. He wasn't asking for much. He just wanted to know that the spark he felt between them was more than just a bit of fun to break up the routine of their days. If he was just a way to pass some time for her, that was okay, too. He didn't have to expect more. He just needed to get a handle on which direction they were going. Sometimes, it was hard to tell with her. That was half the reason he kept chasing Sally's smile. Being unsure if he'd caught it yet gave him a thrill.

Cricket song mingled in the early morning mist outside his door. Peter chuckled as the mist swept past his feet only to disappear in the light cast by the hall lamp. Ghostly visitations. That's what the people of Adington called the wisps when they ventured inside. If there was any truth at all to that claim, Peter hoped his morning guests did more than dance on the threshold and melt beneath the light. He had a long day ahead. It would be nice to come home to supper on the table for a change. Surely some enterprising spirits could manage that if they put their minds to it.

"Run on ahead, Duke. Take Squire with you." He tossed the ball out into the darkness knowing that today wouldn't provide as much time as he would have liked for some pre-dawn play with the dogs. "Don't make a nuisance of yourselves before I catch up. I don't have time to placate anyone over muddy pawprints or slobbery greetings today. We've got rounds to make and pheasants to see to before we start setting up for Mr. Noble's Saturday shoot."

Switching off the lamp, Peter took a minute to let his eyes adjust to the darkness before stepping out. His day had officially begun.

In truth, it had begun a year ago when Mr. Noble offered him the gamekeeper's position. Peter, like everyone who lived and worked on the estate, was on call no matter the hour. That was one of the things he loved about the place. When something went wrong, everyone pulled together to see it put right. The owner of the estate was no exception. Peter knew beyond the shadow of a doubt that his employer would come running in his nightshirt if the need arose. He had seen it happen with his own eyes when the stable hand sent word that one of the mares was in trouble. It was all hands-on deck, John Noble covered in just as much grime as the rest of them by the end of it. The man also sat with the mare and her colt for the rest of the night just to see that they both pulled through the birthing ordeal. Peter's admiration for his employer only rose after that.

That same kind of attitude extended to the village of Adington. Back in the day, it had all been one property with the lord holding it together from the big house where the Noble family now lived. The village was sold off to those who built their lives there over a century ago. If anything, that just made the community knit tighter together around the remnants of the estate that had birthed it. The Nobles might still carry the ancient title handed down through the generations, but at their heart, they were business owners like nearly everyone else in Adington. By working together, the area ran smoothly and prospered as it was meant to. John Noble understood that as much as everyone else. He was kind. He was fair. He just happened to have a bigger roof to care for and a larger plot of land to maintain.

Peter's cottage, now a dark shadow against the hazy first light of a new day, was still a part of the original estate. It shouldered up to the large woods giving him easy access to the wild areas beyond it. John Noble promised that the cottage too would be cut from the main property and sold into Peter's hands if he wanted it, and he planned to spend his life there doing the job the Nobles had been hired him to do. Maybe then Peter's mind would settle into the idea of marriage. Sally had already been hinting about rings. If she could wait another four years for one, he might just buy it for her. That was how long he and the Nobles had agreed on. Both sides saw it as a good space to let Peter get a solid feel for the future he wanted. He would be almost twenty-nine then. Sally would barely be twenty-five. There would still be plenty of time for them to settle down and start a family.

Peter's thoughts turned back to his red-headed sweetheart as he wound through the Footpaths that circled toward the town and the river that bordered it. It was still early days for them in his mind. Less than a year ago he hadn't even known her name. She was just the pretty girl behind the counter at her parents' bakery.

He was still new enough to Adington when he

met her to more often be talked about once a door closed behind him than to be talked to when he was in the room. Sally had changed that with one smile. His heart quickened at the memory. One minute, he was passing the time talking to a couple of the local men about a possible poacher in the area. The next, he felt like he'd been struck by lightning. Every sense he had come alive in the spotlight of Sally's attention. She'd said his name twice before he realized it wasn't just wishful thinking on his part that she knew it. Nothing about that moment in time felt real to this day.

Squatting to check a line of tracks and making a mental note of the deer that left them, Peter's brow knit. What was it about the girl that had him tripping over his words that day? He had never been shy. Observant, sure. That brought out a sort of quiet in a man sometimes. And he spent a lot of time on his own at work. He wasn't much for talking to the trees, so he saved his words unless the dogs were with him. The thing was, on his own, Peter was up for a conversation and a good laugh no matter who the company might be. There was something about Sally that made him fade back so she could shine brighter when he was with her. Ever since that first smile, she was the one who led the conversation. Her tinkling laugh was the signal that pulled his out.

"Maybe that's what I like most about her?" he rationalized as he continued the first leg of his rounds on the way to gather the dogs and spend a few precious moments with the red-headed vixen that kept nosing through his thoughts before stealing a kiss and being on his way to the pheasant pens. "She does all the work for me. I barely even need to think around her. She's happy enough just letting me sit back and stare at her pretty face while she handles everything else."

Was that so bad? There were plenty of men around to talk about the stuff that mattered to him over a pint on a rainy evening. He had friends who were up for casting a line in the water when the weather looked right for a good catch. He didn't lack opportunities to throw on a jersey and battle it out on the pitch when he had the time. So, what if he found himself letting Sally take the lead when they were together? They mostly hung out with her friends, anyway. None of them could tell a deer track from a fox print any more than Peter could name any of the people on their favourite radio show. He didn't have time for that sort of thing. If he turned the radio on in his cottage in the evening it was with the hope that the weatherman would get the next day's forecast right.

"A penny for your thoughts," Sally's musical words brought Peter up short. How had he already reached the village? What had he missed on the way? Sally's smile didn't falter. If anything, it grew even brighter when she saw his confusion. "Were they about me?"

"Always," he just wasn't sure that she would be keen on the direction they took most of the time.

"All is right in the world then." Sally's smile set off a mischievous twinkle in her eye that made Peter's heart skip a beat. "Out here, anyway. Inside is a different story altogether. Dad has got the ovens so hot the devil himself would be begging for ice water if he stepped in the kitchen this morning. Mum is busy sweeping the spirits out before we open as if some fog could be anything of the sort," her blue eyes rolled and fluttered. She sighed to remind them both that she was far too sophisticated to believe in such nonsense. "She swept me right out with them. I did manage to grab a pecan muffin on my way, though. Your slobbering hounds will have to fend for themselves this morning."

Sally held the perfectly baked muffin out to him just as Peter imagined Eve would have done with the apple back when Eden thrived. He took it as Sally scanned the immediate area and then gave a very satisfied smile when she didn't see Duke or Squire loping over to put their muddy paws on her dress. She wore lemon yellow this morning. The shop apron that would cover it was likely folded neatly on the counter still. Her hair was loose and curling around her shoulders daring him to touch its perfect waves. Peter knew better. Sally's perfection wasn't something she took lightly. She would cut their morning short just so she could gather those curls into a tail before taking her place at the counter. There would be a matching lemony ribbon tied into a bow to hold it and somehow the multitude of waves would join as one tidy spiral cascading from it.

"Walk with me to the bridge?" Peter knew it was a long shot. Sally rarely let him take her farther than the bench on the corner unless her friends were along. "We can watch the sun come up over the water."

"And I can be late to work causing Mum to mutter at me instead of the morning fog, you mean." Her smile softened the sting a bit but not entirely. "No thank you, Peter Marsh. She is already in a mood because the big house wants to add to their order. I don't need her snipping at me, too."

"I've never seen your mum snip at a soul," Peter knew he had overstepped as soon as Sally's pretty face scrunched up in a scowl.

"You've never paid attention, then," even her pout was pretty. How was that possible? "She gets in a sour mood just like everyone else. She's just good at hiding it."

"If you say so," Peter shrugged before bending down and touching her nose with his. He gave her a huge smile hoping it would lure hers back. When it didn't, he crossed his eyes and gave her a loud kiss.

"Peter!" A rosy blush lit Sally's cheeks as she tried her best to look offended. The satisfied twinkle in her eye made the rest a lie. "Someone will see!"

"Let them!" He kissed her again for good measure. "I want everyone to see. You're my girl. I should have the right to show that off, don't you think?"

"I think that if I'm your girl, you should ask me to come up to the big house for Saturday's pheasant shoot. Surely, the Noble's amazing gamekeeper is allowed to bring a guest," her big blue eyes turned all soft and innocent and Peter felt himself melting into them.

"I'll be working the whole time," Peter cringed when her pout deepened, and he had to remind himself that cupping her face in his calloused hands would only make things worse. "You would be on your own if I took you. Mister Noble's got an older crowd coming for this one. You wouldn't have much fun. I'm pretty sure Sarah and Jane are trying to figure out whether having games set up is worth the effort. Unless you want to spend the afternoon fanning yourself with a bunch of old ladies while they nibble sandwiches and gossip about people you don't know, I'd say you are better off spending the day with your friends at the park like usual. You'll have more fun there."

"You could always sneak away. It's not like the pheasants will notice. I'm sure there are other people there who can point out where to shoot. And you could get dressed up for a change. We could be the couple that everyone there is whispering about behind their hands. Wouldn't that be fun?" Sally put on her best smile. It was the one that Peter wanted most to catch and tuck in his pocket.

"Maybe you should talk to the Noble daughters if you'd like to go," Peter said wishing that the three of them got along well enough for that to have already been a natural conclusion. "I have a job,

Sally. If I want a future here, I have to do that job right. I can't play dress-up instead. Just like you can't walk to the river with me because you'll be late for work if you do."

"Fine. I should go, anyway. Mum will be ready to start setting things out for the day, I'm sure. She's expecting someone from the big house to come around this morning and finalize the order for the party. That just leaves me to handle the counter." Her chin was raised a bit. Why did it always make Peter feel small when she did that? "Besides, I'm sure you have work of your own to be off to. Walking the Footpaths with your smelly dogs or staring at the ground or something. You better be going."

"Sally, don't be that way," he touched her hand, and she pulled it away. "At least give me a smile before I go."

Her lips tipped into something that might have been a smile if it wasn't so angry. Her blue eyes held the shimmer of unshed tears.

"I'm not the bad guy here, Love," except he still felt like he was the biggest villain in one of her radio shows. "I'll make it up to you on our next day off. We'll go wherever you want."

"I'll bet it won't have a string quartet or be an excuse to wear one of those fancy hats, will it?" Sally sighed. "But I guess that's the best you can do so it's what I'll have to settle for. Go play with your birds, Peter. I'm sure I'll see you again before the big party. Maybe you'll have figured out some way for me to come by then."

She turned and stomped away before Peter could say anything more. The lemon yellow of her skirt swayed in time to the bouncing curls at her shoulders. Peter suddenly felt more ashamed than he thought reasonable. He would show her, though. Even if it meant his next wages, his beautiful Sally would have her string quartet and a reason to wear some silly hat.

"You're still wasting your time with that pretentious piece of fluff, then?" A lovely, feminine voice that sounded even more let down with him than Sally floated out of the fog. Jane Noble. It had to be Jane. The girl turned up at all the worst times. It was like she was always lurking just out of sight waiting to call him out on some new failing. "I thought you would have outgrown that chase by now. Some vixens just can't be caught, Gamekeeper. Haven't you learned that by now?"

"Stop being mean, Jane," try as he might to be respectful to his employer's oldest daughter, Jane Noble made it hard. She spoke her mind far too freely every time she opened her mouth. Since she was out on the estate's acres nearly as much as he was, he got an earful of her opinion whenever their paths crossed. Lately, that happened more than ever before. "What are you doing here, anyway?"

"Oh, Daddy's trying to make a proper lady of me as usual," Jane appeared out of the fog and leaned against the wall of the bakery beside him. She wore denim trousers tucked into boots that had seen better days along with a flannel shirt that was tied at her waist instead of being tucked in. A cap much like Peter's hid all but the bottom chin-length fringe of her dark hair. As always, mischief shined in her jade-green eyes. Turning Jane Noble into any sort of proper lady was a job that Peter firmly believed was far beyond anyone's capabilities. She was a tomboy through and through. Half the men of the village couldn't set a snare as expertly as she could. Most weren't willing to brave the thorns in the thickets she set them in, either. "He seems to believe that sending me to handle orders for the weekend is a good start to that. Who am I to argue?"

"That is between you and your father. Speaking of Mr. Noble," Peter tried to step around her but she outmanoeuvred him in one fluid motion, setting herself directly in his path. "I've got to get back to work. If you'll excuse me?"

It wasn't that he didn't like the eldest Noble daughter. Truth be told, he could easily find the girl comfortable to be around if he didn't know better than to let that happen. Which, he did, Peter reminded himself. His employer's daughter was off-limits in any sort of way. They weren't friends. They couldn't be friends. She needed to stop trying to be friendly with him. He needed to stop falling for the bait on days like today when she did her best to rile him up. He liked his place on the estate far too much to let her jeopardize his job on a lark.

"You deserve someone who appreciates you, Peter Marsh," Jane sang her declaration loud enough that he was sure Sally heard her from inside the bakery.

Peter cringed and kept walking. Two women who got along as well as oil and water both making him feel like he was doing something wrong in one morning was too much. Why couldn't John Noble have sent Sarah? She was sensible. She was a lady if Peter had ever seen one. Jane was just short of feral.

The fog was burning off by the time he made it to the river to collect his two most loyal and reasonable companions. The fact both dogs were soaking wet and half covered in mud didn't change his opinion of them. Duke and Squire knew how to have fun when they found it but that didn't mean they wouldn't focus on the job at hand now that their morning romp was over. They knew their place in Adington just like Peter did.

"Time to earn our keep, boys," Peter picked up the ball that had been dropped at his feet and tucked it into his pocket. Let's go check the trees for those nasty foxes."

Nobody would ever convince him that his dogs didn't understand every word he said. At the mention of foxes, they both went still to sniff the air. Then, it was noses to the ground once they hit the Footpaths again. The woods were thick enough that Peter kept his torch on until they reached the first clearing. He surveyed the location to make sure nothing had changed since yesterday and then let the early morning light show him the space as nature intended.

This was where he would set up the shooting area. It was far enough from the estate's pretty lawn to ensure that the ladies enjoying their afternoon tea there wouldn't be bothered but not so much of a hike that the fine gentlemen would find it a nuisance to walk to. He and the local boys would deliver the pheasants early in the morning and flush them out of the brush when the time was right. A few lucky birds would rejoin the pens by evening but it was Peter's job to ensure that all participants walked away feeling accomplished. One lucky shooter would claim the day's grand prize by taking the biggest bird. Bragging rights and a good bottle of scotch - often shared with the other participants - always added something special that kept Mr. Noble's paying guests coming back for more.

Peter's thoughts turned back to Sally before he could stop them. His beautiful girl was built for afternoon tea in a fancy dress so much more than Jane was. She would be right at home sipping from the dainty China cups and nibbling on finger sandwiches. Mr. Noble would never have felt the need to try to make a lady of Sally had she been born to him instead of the baker. Jane, on the other hand, would put on the dress, powder her nose, and still somehow look like she would be more at home beating the bushes with the boys than whispering behind her gloved hand beside the roses.

Would it be overstepping to have a word with Sarah, the younger Noble daughter, about inviting Sally as a favour to him? Sarah might even find it refreshing to have another girl near her age around.

One that wouldn't need to have an eye kept on her through the whole party, no less. Jane was always getting into some sort of trouble at these things. Sally would be perfectly pleasant. Maybe having her there would help. It was something to consider.

Squire barked, reminding Peter that his considerations needed to be constrained to the job at hand. He went to investigate and found nothing more than some rabbit droppings for his trouble. Rabbits, he could live with. Their season was coming soon enough. Until then, they were more than welcome to multiply to their hearts' content so long as they stayed out of the kitchen gardens.

That reminded Peter that he needed to finalise his choices for Saturday's pheasant butchers. Somehow, the job of hiring them landed in his lap instead of the cook's this time. It was a new responsibility and one not to be taken lightly. He also wanted to talk to one of the local men who had a talent for making arrows. Some of the feathers might be put to good use as fletching. It was another potential revenue stream for Adington and one that saw to it that nearly all of the byproducts of the hunt were put to good use.

As he finished his rounds and headed to the pens, Peter saw Jane stomping back up the lane to the house. Peter shook his head. At eighteen, Jane Noble should be beyond the stomping age. She should be refining her feminine charms and trading in her scruffy boots and flannel for an outfit that might catch her a husband. She didn't lack in looks. Peter, along with every other young man in Adington had to agree that she was pretty as a picture. The girl just couldn't seem to get her head around the idea that it was time to settle down and start a family. It was a shame, all around. The right man would enjoy having a wife he could fish with even if she did tend to catch more than he did. Those men just didn't exist in her social sphere. Jane Noble would have to give up all of her wild ways if she was going to attract one of them.

As if she felt Peter's eyes on her, she turned and made a B-line toward the shed where he stood watching her.

"First off, I would like to say that your sweetheart is probably going to make your ears blister the next time she sees you. It isn't my fault. So don't blame me when it happens. I was told to ask her if she would like to help serve tea to the old biddies on Saturday. She took offense to the idea. Then her mother had a few words with her which only seemed to make things worse. Somehow, you are to blame by default. Don't ask me to explain that because I can't. The long and short of it is that she agreed to pretend she's not seething with mad fury while she carries a tray but told me to tell you that she fully expects you to make it all up to her, whatever that means." Jane threw her hands up like she was hoping for some divine explanation for the whole situation. "And since when did I become her messenger? I swear to you, Peter Marsh. Pretty or not, that girl is going to bring you nothing but heartache if you keep chasing after her. You'll die a penniless fool long before you gain even the smallest sliver of her heart...if she has one. Cut her loose and count yourself lucky if she flies away. You deserve better even if you're too blind to see the truth that's right in front of your face."

Jane threw her hands up one last time and turned on her heel before Peter could get a proper response in order. By the time he found words that wouldn't put him deeper into a hole he didn't remember digging, she was halfway to the house.

Duke's wet nose nudged at his hand. When Peter looked down, the Labrador's big, soulful eyes told him that he wasn't the only one confused.

"It's okay, boy. Lady Jane isn't upset with us. Well, at least not with you," shaking his head, Peter opened the shed door and began filling a bucket with feed. "As for me? Well, maybe she'll stay out of my way for a bit if she's decided I'm to blame for her cranky mood. That, at least, would be a nice change."

As for Sally, well, at least she would get to come to the party, right? Maybe it wouldn't be just how she had imagined it but Peter was sure that she would see that making a bit of extra money while she was there would be a lot more interesting than socializing with a bunch of stuffy old ladies. Still, he made a mental note to check his savings and see if he could arrange a fancy lunch date in the city. It was probably going to take more than that to soothe his fiery red-headed girl after what he was sure she saw as a huge slight. In Sally's mind, nothing was quite so bad as being the hired help when she felt like she should have been a guest instead.

Peter would never understand that. He was happy with his life. He took pride in the work he did. He understood his place in the world and wanted nothing more than what he had. Nothing except for Sally, anyway. And if he ended up a penniless fool like Jane said and never gained Sally's love in return? Well, the chase would have still been worth it in his eyes.

CHAPTER

TWO

The low-slung branch of the tree where Jane sat gave her the perfect view of both her family home and the shady woods that tightened up a stone's throw from where it grew. It was her favourite spot to think. The pull of nature and the tug of family obligations felt more balanced here as if they could peacefully co-exist instead of being constantly at odds with each other. Jane needed that peace today.

It was over a week since what her father had taken to calling The Incident. He said it in a tone that implied that it was only the latest in a string of catastrophes that Jane was solely to blame for setting in motion. To be fair, Jane couldn't exactly argue his logic. Not this time, nor any of the others that he brought up while giving her yet another lecture on ladylike behaviour. According to John Noble, Jane had none to speak of and what little effort she put into faking a well-bred feminine demeanour fell considerably short of the mark.

Scowling at the big house she had grown up in, Jane considered her options. On the one hand, she could send out the innumerable apology notes her father ordered that she write. She could take his suggestion about including a little white lie that implied she had been on cold medication when she had finally had enough of being asked when she was going to get married and snapped. The women demanding her answer were all stuffy old bats. Saying so out loud should have made them feel like their efforts to be such were not in vain. Instead, there was an uproar that resulted in Jane being extricated from the kerfuffle and whisked away where she couldn't do more damage by her oh-so-perfect little sister, Sarah. If anyone should be embarrassed by the events that transpired, it was Jane herself. Besides, she had said at the outset that she didn't want to attend the gathering of fussy old women. Sarah had seconded the idea of handling it solo. But no. She had been forced to put on the fancy dress and sip tea anyway.

If Jane was forced to be involved at all, she should have been allowed to lead the shoot as she had suggested more than once. Why her father insisted that she miss out on the only part of the day that held any interest at all for her was beyond logic. Which brought Jane to her other option. She could let the biddies chirp on about her failings with no hope of an apology that Jane felt they had no right waiting for and get on with being herself. If her dear father couldn't accept her for who she was, that was just going to have to be his problem, wasn't it?

Turning away from the sprawling house, Jane stared out into the cool shadows of the wood. That was where she belonged. She understood the way of things there. She could walk the paths blindfolded and never misstep. She could stalk a deer so quietly that she could almost brush its twitching hide before it ran. The rabbits for the cook's pot had no place to hide. Jane knew their ways far too well for that. As for the fish, they only stood a chance if Jane was in the mood to throw them back once she caught them.

Jane knew who she was among the trees. Well, nearly so. There was one little part that made no rational sense. That was how her heart skipped a beat whenever she sensed that Peter Marsh was near.

He was tall. He was handsome. He was living the life that she longed to live. That might be enough for some girls. Then again, some girls wanted to be married. They wanted to giggle and bat their eyes until some poor, unsuspecting boy tripped over his own feet and landed on one knee. They wanted to start popping out babies and talking about new curtains for the dining room. Jane wanted more out of life than nappies and pot roast for dinner. She wanted...

...She wanted Peter Marsh. Just thinking about life beside him as he walked the Footpaths and cared for the creatures that called the estate's wood home made her feel free. They would make a good match, she and Peter. If he could get his head around it, that is. Right now, the man was all starry-eyed over the prissy baker's daughter. That girl, Sally, would make him miserable, of course. That was a given. Deep down, Peter had to know that.

Without thinking about it, Jane slipped down from the tree and headed for the nearest trail. Checking the sun, she smiled. Peter was a creature of habit just like the rest of the woodland animals. All she had to do was meander her way toward the pheasant pens and she would run into him on his afternoon rounds of the estate. She would taunt him a bit and he would do his best to be polite. Then, when she hit the right nerve, he would switch gears and pretend indifferent toward her. That's when she knew she had won their little game.

One day, she would break through that, too. One day, her father's gamekeeper would finally have a moment when he forgot that she was the boss's daughter and say what was really on his mind. She longed for that time nearly as much as the butterflies in the pit of her stomach craved an excuse to take flight at his nearness. One day, Peter Marsh would see her as the woman she was and understand that they were meant for each other. Then, he would stop worrying that her father wouldn't approve. He would stop chasing after silly Sally. Jane was patient. That didn't mean she was going to give up on her prize. Not even a little bit. Peter was in her sights. It was only a matter of time before she caught him fair and square.

Right on schedule, Duke and Squire rounded a bend and loped over to her. She took a couple of treats from her pocket and offered them along with a laughing romp that she knew delighted the dogs almost as much as it did her.

"There are my good boys!" she said squatting down so they could bathe her cheeks in wet kisses. "Oh, there they are! Have you been chasing those bad old foxes?"

"They were on the trail of one, although I'm sure now they've forgotten all about it," Peter gave her a long-suffering look. "You shouldn't distract them during working hours, Jane. They have a job to do."

"Oh, one little treat and a good scratch behind the ears never hurt anyone, Peter," Jane smoothed Duke's cheeks, planted a kiss on his head, and turned to do the same for Squire. "Besides, I just came up the trail. The only thing that might interest these two was a pheasant that is still eluding capture after the shoot."

Peter opened his mouth as if to say something and snapped it closed again, his jaw muscles tightening. He took a deep breath and let it out before giving her a polite smile.

"Stop doing that, would you?" Jane interrupted before the man could say whatever ridiculously courteous nonsense he was about to spout. The sour mood brewing inside her all day amped up its effect on her attitude. "I believe it is a well-established fact that I am not the lady of the manor around here. Stop treating me like I'm somehow less than human.

I'm sick of it. I'm sick of all of it. I am not some China doll that will shatter into pieces if you say the wrong word or use a less-than-pleasant tone. If you can't see that, Peter Marsh, maybe you should retrain Duke and Squire to be your eyes as well as your nose."

The words were out before she could stop them. It was as if all of her annoyance finally demanded a vent.

"Jane, be reasonable," his tone was meant to be placating but Jane could only hear her father using the same words an hour ago. It was too much.

"I *am* being reasonable. As a matter of fact, I seem to be the only one around here who has any reason inside their brain. Everyone else is determined to force me into a role that I can't play. Look at me, Peter. No, really look. I am not Sarah with her refinement and dreams of being the lady of the house. I'm not even Sally with her ambition to be more than she is. I'm Jane. Just Jane. I want the smell of the earth after a good rain. I want the sunset with my hook in the water and my bare feet in the mud. I want to lure a swarm of bees into a hive box so I can collect honey and lick it off my fingers. I want to laugh with the foxes and scurry through the thickets with the rabbits. Why is that asking so bloody much?" Tears stung her eyes. Jane wasn't sure if they were from desperate sadness or rage. It didn't matter. The look on Peter's face said it all. She had finally given voice to the pain inside and he was horrified at her candour. "You'll never understand. Nobody will."

She ran before the one man in all of the world who might be able to see her if he took off his blinders could feel forced to come up with some new, horribly civil response. She couldn't hear it. Not now. Not ever. Her heart would break into a thousand pieces and take her strong will with it into oblivion. She needed to be alone. She needed to find the peace this wood always gave her.

She didn't stop until she reached the clearing where she should have been last Saturday instead of at the miserable tea where everything had gone so wrong. It was getting dark. The moon already rose to dapple the soft grass with its reflected light. Her cap was lost somewhere back along the path she had cut through the underbrush. Sweat made the scratches on her arms sting. Taking the first full breath she had managed since her outburst, Jane sat down on the grass wishing it could swallow her.

"You must think I'm nothing but a spoiled ninny," Jane said a few minutes later when the crickets went silent announcing an intruder to her solitude. She could all but feel Peter's presence. Duke and Squire came to sit beside her seconds later. She took the cap Squire held in his between his teeth and crammed it back onto her head.

"I think you're having a bad day, Jane. Nothing more," Peter spoke quietly as if doing his best not to spook some wounded animal. "Let me walk you home."

"I can find my way," Jane's chin lifted in the growing darkness. She had to be stubborn now. It wasn't her way home she was talking about. It was her life. If she couldn't convince herself that she knew the right path for her future, how was she ever going to convince anyone else? "Just go. I'll be fine."

"Don't make things harder than they have to be, Jane. Let me see you home. I want to keep my head firmly on my shoulders and my job as gamekeeper here, as well." At least Peter wasn't trying to sound reasonable or polite now. That was something, right? "I can't just leave you out here at night and go back to my cottage for tea. If you won't think about your well-being, maybe you can think about mine."

"You don't have to say that you saw me at all. I'm not one of your pheasants. You have no reason to know where I am at any given moment." If he would just look at her the way he looked at Sally, she would agree that her whereabouts were his business. Until that happened, he could go away.

"They are your father's pheasants as much as you are his daughter and I am his employee. It is as much, if not more, my duty to see that you are safe as it is to see that the birds are fed and kept from harm," Peter was being reasonable again although there was a sharp edge to it now. When she didn't answer, he threw up his hands and finally lost his temper. "Jane Noble, stop behaving like a child. You are at an age where you need to grow up. If you won't do it for your father or your sister or anyone else that cares about you, do it for yourself. If you want everyone to stop treating you like a spoiled ninny, stop behaving like one."

Jane was speechless. Never, in all of her many imaginary dealings with Peter Marsh had she expected quite that sort of response from him. She wasn't sure whether she should be offended or impressed. Finally, he had spoken to her as if she was a person just like he was instead of some great lady he had to bow and scrape for. It made her heart soar even while she blushed with shame.

"You are right, of course," she said with as much dignity as she could muster. She wasn't sure she had ever actually felt contrite before. The feeling was alien to her. Wild, temperamental, and exquisitely rebellious were things she knew. This was something different. No one but Peter could have made her so embarrassed by her behaviour. It was sobering. "Will you give me a hand up?"

When his strong, calloused hand closed around hers, she knew beyond the shadow of a doubt that it was the only one she was ever going to willingly hold. He pulled away so quickly once she was on her feet that she knew he felt something, too. He looked away so she couldn't see what that something was. That was enough to tell her that a spark had ignited between them. Why else would he be so careful not to brush against her as they began walking back along the path toward the big house? Why else would he be so awkward about holding the occasional whip of underbrush out of the way?

When they reached the stone walkway leading to the door of her father's home, Peter nodded once and turned on his heel as if his duty was finished and he could finally escape her presence. She wasn't fooled. Her heart was beating too fast at the thought of him walking away for the swell of feelings to be hers alone.

"Peter?" Jane wanted to ask him if he thought he

could love her just a little. If he could care for her just enough to let her be who she was instead of insisting that she be someone else entirely. Instead, when he stopped but would not face her, she said, "Thank you."

He nodded again before walking back into the night with the dogs at his side. Jane stood watching him until he was lost to the shadows. Finally, she slipped quietly into the house and up to her room.

A soft knock sounded at the door. Sarah. No one else would have noticed Jane's arrival, so it had to be her.

"Come in," Jane sighed. She loved her sister dearly but right now, she just wanted to be alone with her thoughts of Peter.

"You missed your supper," Sarah, always so poised that Jane had to wonder how they were related at all, balanced a tray as she entered. "Don't worry. Daddy just thinks you are sulking after this afternoon's talk."

"Lecture, you mean." Jane flopped back on her bed and stared at the ceiling as Sarah set the tray down. "It's always a lecture and I'm not invited to say anything at all."

"Have you considered that he may have a point?" Sarah pulled the chair from the dressing table to the side of the bed and sat down as prim and proper as one of the tea guests. She was a lovely thing, all peaches, and cream with soft dark curls and eyes as big and brown as a doe. In a couple of years, the girl would become breathtakingly beautiful. Combined with her quiet demeanour and innate charm, Sarah Noble was the perfect example of a lady if there ever was one.

"I don't need this from my younger sister, too," Jane huffed out a breath. "I am who I am Sarah. I'm never going to be like you. Getting married and having babies isn't anywhere near the top of my list of things to do. Neither is playing hostess or planning events around a bunch of people I want nothing to do with. You are wonderful at all of those things. I'm never going to be. Why can't everyone just accept that and let me be who I am? I'm good at a great many things. They just aren't girly. If I was a son instead of a daughter, this would be a completely different conversation."

"But you aren't," Sarah pointed out. "Like it or not, Daddy's expectations for you are the same as they are for me. One day, you'll see the joy of being a wife and mother. I'm sure you will. And it's not like you need to find a man who wants you to powder your nose and giggle your way through life. There are plenty of them out there who would find your interests to fit well with their own. You just need to compromise a bit and be pleasant through the rest of it. That's all."

"How many men in our social circle take any interest at all in stalking deer or catching fish unless it's a planned outing where the creatures are delivered right to them by people who actually know what they're doing in the great outdoors?" That was the entire problem as far as Jane saw it. She was going to be stuck with some soft-handed fool of a husband who thought that the whole world should be made tame for him. The wildness that lived within her would be the first casualty of their marriage. The thought made her feel physically ill.

"I'm sure the right man is out there, Jane." Sarah smoothed her palms across the dainty floral pattern of her skirt, signalling that she had said her peace and was about to leave. "Compromise, Jane. That is how life works. You will be a lot happier once you accept that and get some practice using it. I will help you as much as I can, of course, but you are still going to have to be the one who does the work. All Daddy needs is to see that you are trying. That will set his mind at ease. He's just worried about you, is all."

"I suppose you are right," Jane said just to end the conversation and regain the privacy of her room. Somewhere in the back of her mind, the whisper of a thought was taking shape. She wasn't quite sure what it would look like in the end but if Sarah didn't leave, the faint idea trying to form was liable to disappear faster than fog on a sunny morning. "Thank you, Sarah. And thank you for not telling anyone I wasn't in my room this evening. I just needed some time to think away from the house. I didn't mean to be gone so long. And for my supper. I wasn't even aware that I was hungry at all until you brought it."

"That's what sisters are for," Sarah smiled brightly as if she had just solved the final problem plaguing the world. "I'll see you at breakfast. Maybe afterward, we could go shopping."

"If you would like," Jane gave Sarah her best smile. They both knew she hated shopping trips but if it would make Sarah believe she was going to try her best to become the woman everyone else wanted, so be it.

When Jane was alone again, she got up to pace. Compromise. That's what Sarah kept going on about. All Jane needed to do was find a way to be herself and still fulfil the great John Noble's expectations for his eldest daughter's future. Either that or find a way to slip out from under them without causing too much of a ruckus.

She didn't have the means to simply leave home and build a life of her own. That left marriage as her only option. But who to tie herself to? None of the papered sons of her father's peers appealed in the slightest. She would make them just as miserable as they would make her. Anyone outside of that tight and titled circle would be scandalous to entertain. Then again, scandals eventually faded into the background. There was always a new one on the horizon to occupy the elite ladies' need for good gossip.

Jane paused to look out the window at the midnight moon. Hadn't she been told more than once that she was scandalous? Hadn't she already been the topic of whispered conversations over fine China tea sets? Perhaps one last uproar was just the thing to solve her problem. An unequal marriage wasn't unheard of, after all. How long could everyone carry on about it? She would be safely out of the limelight. No one would feel the need to invite her to their socials because she would be an outcast. That meant no one would need to worry that she might embarrass them with her behaviour. Surely, they would grow bored quickly. Then, everyone could get back to their lives and breathe a sigh of relief that her antics wouldn't disrupt them any further.

Peter came instantly to mind causing Jane's heart to leap. He was perfect. She was already half in love with him and certain that he had at least some affection for her. He was above reproach as far as his reputation in the village. As gamekeeper of her father's estate, it seemed reasonable that Jane might take a shine to him. Everyone knew she was more than rebellious enough to let herself fall for a handsome man living close enough to bump into daily. And why shouldn't she? A life in the cozy cottage where he lived seemed ideal to her. She would still be close enough to home that her father could watch her happiness unfold and see that she had made the right choice. Besides, John Noble truly liked the man he had hired to see to the estate's creatures. How could he not be happy with the match after the shock wore off? He had, after all, hired Peter to handle the wild things within his domain. Why not admit that Jane belonged on that list as well? It was nothing that hadn't been implied before. As a bonus, Jane was sure that Peter Marsh would welcome a wife who appreciated his love of the outdoors instead of finding himself strapped to someone like Sally who would turn her nose up when he came home smelling of the pheasant pens every night. It was a perfect solution for everyone.

Heart pounding in her chest, Jane snuck back out of the house and slipped through the darkness. If she didn't do this now, she might lose her nerve. Peter was her only hope of happiness, and he needed to be made to see that she was his only hope as well. Judging by his reaction to her in the clearing, surely a kiss would open his eyes to the truth of it. If not, she would be relentless in her pursuit of him until he saw the light. It was the only way.

Knocking on the sturdy wooden door of the cottage, Jane held that thought firmly in her frantic mind. Butterflies or not, this was not a time to be soft. She knew beyond the shadow of a doubt what she wanted, and nothing would stop her from getting it. Not her father. Not the threat of being ridiculed again. Not even Peter himself. This key to her future happiness was nothing more than another patient hunt. She would have her prize no matter how long it took.

"Jane? What are you doing here?" Peter looked worried. "Is everything okay? Am I needed?"

"I..." Jane thought fast. Now that he was standing before her with the light from his hall lamp spilling across the threshold between them, she wasn't sure what to do.

"This isn't a time for games, Jane. Is everyone alright?" Peter reached out as if to take her by the shoulders and give her a good shake. At the last second, he pulled his hands back and tucked them in his pockets.

There was only one thing to do. Jane let her eyes flutter and her body went limp. Peter caught her as she fell just as she knew he would. Then he scooped her into his arms and carried her to the couch. She could feel his heart hammering behind his ribs with a tempo that matched hers. Before he could set her down, she slid her arms around his neck and brought her lips to his.

For the barest of seconds, Peter stood frozen. Jane could taste his shock when her lips parted softly against his. Then, his hunger for her kiss drowned it out. She sighed softly as she melted against his solid body. This. This was what she wanted. All of the pieces of the puzzle fell into place. Jane saw the future they would share as the kiss deepened, taking on a life of its own. It was everything she wanted. He was everything she had ever dared to dream of.

"I should go," Jane's words were breathless and husky by the time their lips parted.

"You should," Peter's voice shook. "You shouldn't be here."

He set her down although neither of them let go. Instead, their lips touched again. This time, something far more than simple desire fuelled their kiss. Jane pressed closer willing the man she had chosen to ask for more from her. She would give him everything she had to give. Her life belonged to him now. Her future rested in his work-worn hands.

"Go home," Peter manoeuvred her toward the door even as his lips brushed hers again. "Go home, Jane. You need to leave while I can still close the door behind you."

She left him standing with his hands braced on the doorframe but only because she couldn't think straight any longer. It wasn't until she was back in her room that she realized she had left at all. Touching her swollen lips with her fingertips, she drew in a shaking breath. Everything was different now. She had found her answer, and it was perfect.

But in the morning, instead of the happy smile and passionate embrace she expected, Peter was cold.

"I don't understand," Jane felt tears welling up

when he turned his back and started to walk hurriedly away when she met up with him on the Footpaths during his rounds. "Peter, why are you being like this?"

"Last night was a mistake, Jane," his words came out through gritted teeth. "You have to see that, too. You should have never come to the cottage. I should have never fallen for your antics."

"But that kiss -" Her heart still thrilled at the memory.

"Should have never happened," he insisted. He still wouldn't look at her. "That was a childish prank that you pulled. I'm not sure which one of us should be more ashamed. Go home and grow up. I don't have time for your nonsense."

That stopped Jane in her tracks. How could he think such a thing? She knew he felt the same fire in his veins as she did when they kissed. How could he lie so cruelly now? She couldn't make herself follow as he continued along the trail. Duke and Squire whimpered as their big soulful eyes turned first her way and then toward Peter's hurried retreat. Finally, they left her, too. Jane wrapped her arms across her chest as a chill ran through her soul. She had never felt so alone in her life.

CHAPTER

THREE

"Jane Noble, what do you want from me?" Peter asked three days later when the girl fell into step beside him on his rounds.

Never in his life had Peter struggled so hard to do the right thing. He knew that Jane needed to be kept at arm's length. Farther, if he could manage it, which he couldn't because she made it her mission in life to drive him mad. She appeared around every corner. She lurked at the pheasant pens until he was forced to choose between being near her or starving the birds. She was ever-present, and just as forbidden as she had ever been. Only now he knew what she felt like in his arms. He saw her and could taste her kiss all over again. It was infuriating. Didn't she know that she was turning him inside out? And for what? She was toying with him just for sport. That's all it could be.

"I think that what I want should be obvious, Peter," Jane said softly. Her voice held so much hope that his heart ached with longing. "I want you. I want us. Why is this so hard for you to understand?"

"You want things that can't be." Why couldn't she see reason? She was who she was. He was never going to measure up to the standards required in a suiter. The girl had to know that. "Go find some other poor soul's heart to cut your teeth on. I've no need nor do I have the desire to be the recipient of your attention."

That only seemed to steel her resolve more. Worse, Peter had the feeling that she knew he was lying through his teeth. A week went by with her constant appearances at every turn. Jane brought him lunch. She invaded his favourite fishing hole. She started measuring out the feed for the pheasants and carrying the bucket to the pens to help him feed them. He tried switching up his routine but she caught on with barely a day of peace for his trouble.

The second week, he began watching for her. The moments when they were together stopped feeling awkward. Jane's shadow stretching out beside his became far too normal for the quiet voice of his conscience that constantly warned him about the pitfall of being around her.

By the end of the month, he stopped trying to lie to himself and admitted that he enjoyed having her around. He still knew better than to let her get too close. The memory of her soft lips still haunted him, waking him up in the middle of the night with a need so great it made Peter curse himself for ever coming to Adington. Only in the light of day was John Noble's eldest daughter real enough that he could control those wayward thoughts.

The only place he was safe from Jane's temptation was the village itself. She called her offer to organise and plan the Autumn festival from the estate a compromise. Her father called it a step forward in his efforts to turn his tomboy daughter into a lady. Sarah gladly took on the role of liaison with the shops and vendors who would set up during the fair. Peter thought she looked a little too triumphant about the whole thing but understood better after Jane's cursor explanation of her sister's advice. What he didn't understand was why Jane had suddenly become so willing to follow it.

The one good thing that Jane's strange compliance did was give him a place where he wasn't constantly on his toes waiting for her to turn up. He took advantage of it whenever he could, figuring that eventually the wretched pull Jane had on him would snap and he would be able to put all of the impossible thoughts of her out of his head once and for all.

"Are you even listening to me, Peter?" Sally asked on the first chilly morning of autumn. Her breath was a feathery plume of mist in the cold air between them. "I swear, it's like you are a million miles away today."

"I'm sorry, Sally," he apologized automatically. There had been a great many of these moments lately. Try as he might, the red-haired baker's daughter just couldn't keep his mind from wandering back to Jane. "I was thinking of the harvest festival and what I need to do so the grounds are ready to host everyone."

"I am so tired of hearing about that stupid festival. It's still weeks away and it's all anyone can talk about. We do this every year. It's the same every time. I'm not sure why we need to think of it at all," Sally pouted. "Did you know that I'm expected to man the bakery booth? It's just rude. I want to be able to enjoy myself, too. No one ever thinks of that. They just think they are doing me a favour by offering me money to stand behind a bunch of baked goods. I do enough of that at the bakery all day."

"You have to admit, it is good money, though," Peter reminded her. "The tips alone much add up."

"You sound more and more like mum and dad every day," Sally sounded more angry than hurt. "I don't even know why I spend my time with you."

"I've been wondering the same thing." Peter felt the words coming before they slipped through his lips but couldn't stop them. At Sally's shocked expression, he tried to salvage things. "I didn't mean it like that, Sally. You know I didn't."

"I'm not sure there is any other way you could have meant it, Peter," Sally huffed. "I work all the time. I can't see how I should be expected to work more and be happy about it. Every girl wants a few hours of fun where she can dress up and be special."

Not every girl, Peter thought. Not Jane. She was happier when she had her hands in the work she shouldn't be doing than when she had to get fancy. He pushed the thought away. He had to stop comparing the two girls who were in a secret battle for his attention. He was all too aware that Sally came up short in the contest.

"All I meant was that making some extra money isn't such a bad thing. I'm sure you won't have to work the whole time. I'll plan my breaks to line up with yours so we can walk around together." The thought didn't give him nearly as much pleasure as it once would have.

"I've already decided to skip my breaks and leave early. Once I'm off for the day, I'm going home. I am not going to give anyone the chance to tell me I need to help out any more than I have to. If I'm not there, they can't." Her chin was up again. Once, he thought it made her look regal. Now, he could see the childish temper behind it as she looked at Peter like she was waiting for him to try to coax her into changing her mind.

"Well, I guess if that's what you want to do, it's what is best." He felt the most unwelcome relief. Lately, he felt that every minute with Sally was wasted time. How had he not seen just how spoiled she was before?

"It is." She got up from the bench and started to flounce away. "I'll be too busy in the morning to bring you breakfast. You'll have to make do with whatever you have at the cottage or wait until the bakery is open like everyone else."

Peter knew she was angry. He knew that somehow he had said the wrong thing again. A few weeks ago, that would have bothered him. Now, he was strangely happy that he wouldn't have any reason to come by the bakery tomorrow. It wasn't the first time Sally had told him to get lost in one way or another. He was fairly certain it would prove to be the last. In his heart, Peter knew that he and Sally were over. He wanted more than she had to offer. Deep down, he knew that she would never be content to build a life in the gamekeepers' cottage. Sally firmly believed that she was destined for greater things. He hoped the girl found the life she dreamed of one day. Otherwise, whoever she married was in for a world of misery.

Halfway back to the estate, Peter found Jane frolicking along the river's edge with Duke and Squire. It didn't surprise him. Just because she avoided the village didn't mean she shied away from the outskirts. What did give him a jolt was how seeing her, bundled up against the chill of the morning, made him feel all warm inside.

"You're going to catch your death out here if you keep letting those two shake water on you," even as he said it, Duke splashed his way out of the river with the ball in his mouth and rained cold water all over the laughing object of Peter's inappropriate affections. Jane's laugh was amazing. It was genuine, unlike the twittering giggles of Sally and her friends. Hearing it made Peter want to snatch her up and spin her around before planting a solid kiss on her soft lips.

"As if anyone could accuse me of being a delicate flower prone to fainting spells and the dreaded chills if a draft so much as threatens to touch me. I've got the constitution of an ox, Peter. I haven't been sick a day in my life. Let us have our fun." Jane flashed him a smile that set every nerve ending he owned into a frenzy of delight. "Besides, you were busy. We had to content ourselves with our own company. A game of chase the ball was the only thing that could lift our spirits."

"As if your spirits ever need lifting." He took the ball from her and their fingers brushed. Too late, he saw the error. Making contact of any sort with Jane Noble was a form of torture for him. He threw the ball harder than he needed to and watched the dogs splash into the water after it so he wouldn't have to look at her. "So, what is it today? Did you get sent to the village to deal with festival business or are you just out and about?"

She was silent longer than he was comfortable with, especially since he felt her eyes on him the whole time.

"Truth?" she asked finally.

"Am I going to prefer a lie?" The air around them felt heavier than it should.

"Probably," she admitted with a grin.

"Then maybe you should come up with a good one." Peter could only hope she did. Preferably it would also give him an excuse to get away from her before he gave in to the urge to tuck the stray lock of short dark hair back behind her ear.

"Not today," Jane said softly. "Today I want nothing but truth between us. I was looking for you. I figured you were still trying to convince yourself that your early morning visits with Sally were going somewhere. So, I came to show you they aren't. You were scowling when you found us. Then you smiled like sunshine. Now, you're wishing you could scowl again but for a whole different reason. Peter..."

"Don't say it, Jane. Whatever it is, don't say it." There was only one direction her words could be heading and that led to ground he had no business treading. If she gave voice to the desire he knew full well burned between them, Peter wasn't sure if he could offer up a decent argument.

"We're perfectly suited, you and I." And there it was. The naked truth that could only be their downfall. "We love the same things. We want the same kind of life. We were meant for each other. It's really that simple. Why do you feel the need to make it all so complicated?"

"We are not well suited at all!" Peter started walking. He had to move, had to get away from the arguments she so casually threw at him. "You have no idea what you are saying, Jane. You have no idea at all. I am an employee of your father's estate. You are his eldest daughter. You have a title. I have nothing but the work that I do. I have the respect of a man that I admire. One day, I might be lucky enough to buy the house I live in. That's enough for me. It will never be enough for the Lady Jane Noble. Not in this world or the next. Not in your family's eyes. Not in the eyes of your peers. Stop pretending that it will be and stop trying to tempt me into throwing away my future because you like the daydream you've conjured up. We can't even be friends, Jane. Our positions in life are too unequal."

"Only if you are stupid enough to believe all of that silliness." Jane couldn't quite keep up with his longer stride, but she was still far too close. The only saving grace to the situation was that there was no one around to hear. "Sarah can have my title right along with her own. I have no use for it. As for my peers. Most of them see me and wish they could run away as to still look dignified. All I want is a happy life. All I want is you."

"Stop it, Jane." He wanted to cover his ears like a child so he couldn't hear her. He wanted to run back to his cottage and lock the door. He was a full-grown man, for the sake of all that was good and right in the world. No silly girl's fantasies should make him feel this way. Yet, here he was trying to flee from her as if he had any chance of escape. There was no getting away from her, not even when she wasn't around. Jane had crawled beneath his skin and was quickly burrowing her way into his heart. He couldn't allow it. Yet, here he was trying to stop the insane voice in his head from agreeing with her.

"No." She ran up to block his way once they reached the trees. "I won't stop believing that we would be happy together. I won't stop dreaming of what our life would be. I won't stop until you admit that you see it too. And once you do, I won't stop until that life is a reality. Peter Marsh, be honest. Tell me the truth and don't let all of your worries get in the way of it. Tell me you want me, too."

He had Jane in his arms before he could think. His mouth found hers and he drank her in like a dying man. She had pushed him too far this time. There was no other course of action but to give in to the need he had for her. It was the same need that sang in her kiss.

"You are going to be the death of me, woman." He said softly when he broke the kiss. He should push her away. He should leave Adington before things could go any farther. It wouldn't take him long to pack. He could come up with some sort of excuse to give if he tried. Instead, Peter pressed his forehead to hers and whispered, "Come to the cottage tonight if you haven't regained your senses and seen that this whole thing is a mistake. Come to the cottage and let me make love to you. Let me call you mine even if it is only within those walls. Let me believe that the future you see inside that beautiful, mad skull of yours can be real. We'll both find out soon enough that it can't. Let me have until that happens."

"Let's go now," Jane was breathless. "Let's not wait. I've waited long enough for you to admit that you want me."

"We can't be caught together, Jane. You know that." A shiver ran up his spine at the thought. If she snuck to his door tonight, he would be betraying her father's trust and putting her reputation in jeopardy. She could recover if they took the precaution of keeping their tryst a secret. Peter would lose his job, of course. He would lose the life he had in Adington. He could start over somewhere else if it came to that. Excuses could be made for his leaving. He could live with all of that so long as he didn't crash Jane's life along with his. "This...whatever this is between us, has to stay secret. You have to be smart for your own sake. You've won. Let that be enough. Maybe you'll find your common sense again and stay home instead of claiming your prize. The better part of me hopes you do."

"Liar," she leaned up and kissed him again.

He was and he knew it full well. God help him, Peter wished with all his heart that telling her he hoped she stayed away was the truth. He wished he was strong enough to make it so.

When she came to his door after the sun sank below the horizon and all of the decent people of Adington were tucked away in bed, he let her in. He was a fool for doing so. She was every bit as much of one for being there. Somehow, that didn't matter. By the time she slipped away so no one would find her gone when they woke, it mattered even less.

After that, they couldn't get their fill of each other. Every moment they could steal together was blissful torment. The secret they shared made their affair all the more thrilling. Stolen nights turned into weeks of nocturnal delight. It was only the threat of dawn that put a damper on their passion.

"I want to stay here with you," Jane stretched like a cat as his hand smoothed down her soft skin. "I want to fall asleep in your arms and wake up to your kisses."

"I wish that was something we could have, Jane." More than anything Peter wished that now. Somewhere along the line, the heat between them was softened by something he was all too sure was love. "I wish that forever was something I could promise you."

Peter was still struggling with guilty feelings over what he saw as his betrayal. Everything he had now was because John Noble trusted him. Peter's loyalty was tainted by what he and Jane were doing. His duty to his employer had shadows now where there should be none. Eventually, something would have to give. The waking dream that he and Jane shared would have to end.

Jane knew it, too, although she never said as much. Peter saw her wrestling with the conundrum of her father's expectations for her life and her own wishes about how to live it. She didn't talk about it openly, but Peter always knew when the subject of her future had come up at home. There was a desperation in their lovemaking on those nights as if she was willing the universe itself to bend around her feelings for him.

"One day," she gave him a sad grin. "One day, Peter Marsh, you will be compelled to make an honest woman of me. We'll get married, and I will wake up in this bed every morning so I can grumble about making your coffee. You just wait and see."

Peter wanted to believe her. If that life was possible, he would ask her to marry him right now and have her to the church by noon tomorrow. He knew better. Nobody went to this much trouble to hide a relationship when they knew they could have it out in the open. Not when their feelings were as real as his and Jane's. Deep down, the woman in his arms understood that, too. She had to. There would be no one day for them unless they counted the one that they would have to set each other aside and see reason.

"You better get back before someone notices you're gone," he dropped a kiss between her shoulder blades as he cautioned her. "You need some sleep. We've got an early morning tomorrow. Neither of us wants anyone to ask why we're both yawning in unison while everyone else is excited about setting up for the festival."

"Which reminds me," Jane sat up and began dressing. "Sally has been particularly unpleasant lately. From what I've heard in passing – because I do my best to pass that girl quickly when our paths cross – she feels slighted by your lack of attention over the past weeks. You should really put an official end to your pursuit of her, Peter. Simply not going to the bakery in the mornings and telling her that you are busy with other things when she has a free afternoon doesn't sound like it's good enough. If you are waiting for her to get the hint that things are over between the two of you, I have a feeling she will cause no end of trouble before she admits it to herself. She already doesn't like me much. And she's a nosy little beast. If we aren't willing to let our relationship out into the open, I worry that she will jump to her own conclusions if she sees us together. Women can sense when a man is too familiar with a rival. She is not going to keep the secret for us once she ferrets it out."

"Would you have me set her into fits while we are trying to get the decorations hung up and the entertainment running smoothly, Jane?" This was another thing Peter was wrestling with. He had let the situation with Sally go on too long. There hadn't seemed a good time or a good enough excuse to set things straight with her. Each day that passed made a clean ending less likely now.

"You know what I would have, Peter," Jane gave him a wistful smile. "Barring that, I would have you listen to your conscience. No matter how horrid I think Sally is, even she doesn't deserve to be strung along like this. Can we at least agree that once the festival is over, you will break it off in a manner that she understands? Avoidance doesn't seem to be doing the trick."

"As soon as the festival closes, I'll talk with her," Peter agreed. "To be honest, I didn't think she would even notice that I wasn't hanging around anymore. She didn't have much interest in me aside from fussing about the dogs and my work schedule when I put in the effort. I thought she would have wandered off in search of someone new by now."

"Well, that doesn't seem to be the case," Jane shrugged. "I heard her pouring out her confused little heart all over Sarah the other day while she should have been helping with the decorations. Sarah got so frustrated with it all that she had a most unladylike moment and raised her voice. I haven't heard her do that since we were children. She apologised, of course, and claimed she had a headache. If that was true at all, it most likely came from Sally's constant whining. I said as much. Sarah didn't bother to argue."

"I'll handle it," Peter laid back against the pillow where Jane's scent still lingered. "In the meantime, try to play nice. If you can't manage that, do your best to avoid her. And we will both make sure she doesn't see us together."

"At what point does it become strange that we are taking such pains to not be in the same place at the same time?" Jane was dressed now. Her hair was smoothed as if it had never been mussed by their lovemaking. This was the part of the night that Peter hated. His bed always felt so cold once Jane left it. "We need to sort us out as well once the festival is over. I don't mean to put more pressure on you, but it will have to be done. You know what I want, and I know that you want the same. We need to find a way to make it happen without seeing our fears come to life. My father can be made to understand, Peter. I know he can. He's a good man even if he wants all the wrong things for me. He respects you. He will see the positive side of our being a couple once he has a moment or two to let the idea settle. We both need to stop expecting the worst of a man who has never been cruel a day in his life."

That was the crux of it for Peter. What Jane said

was true. John Noble was a good man. No one could deny that. What a good man was capable of doing when it came to protecting those he loved was a whole different story. Even the best father and the most decent of men could be pushed too far. The idea of Jane losing her place in this world to marry so far beneath her was something that could make him stumble hard. Peter didn't want to see what that looked like. He didn't want Jane to know that the man who had given her life and indulged nearly every whim she had while she grew up could become someone she didn't even know if the circumstances were right.

"We'll talk more after the festival," Peter said knowing that it had to be done but that the outcome might not be what either of them wanted. "Until then, we should probably keep to our own beds." When Jane sighed, he added, "It's only a few days. We'll both be busy so the time will fly. Once it's over and Sally has been officially set free, we can sort things out between us and come up with a plan."

"I hate it when you are reasonable, you know," Jane leaned down to give him one last, lingering kiss. "But I do see your point. Besides, what is a few days compared to the lifetime I plan to spend with you?"

When the cottage door clicked closed behind the woman Peter was falling desperately in love with, he got up to make himself a cup of tea. He didn't like complications of this magnitude. Right now, there were far too many and they wound too tightly around his soul, threatening everything he held dear.

Not for the first time, he considered suggesting that he and Jane run off. They could start over somewhere new; somewhere that who they were didn't matter nearly as much as it did here. The idea wasn't cowardly, he told himself. He was being practical. Jane might not care for her reputation now but one day it could and should matter. Perhaps it was better to begin their life together at a distance. That way, everyone would have time to forget about the hurt they would cause in the building of their future together. If John Noble never forgave him for stealing his eldest daughter, Peter could live with that. The idea shamed him but in the bigger picture, Peter knew his feelings were unimportant. He needed to know that Jane would not suffer the loss of her family if they dared to pursue their love for each other.

Fingers of fog drifted across the floor as if reaching for him. The season was changing fast and he hadn't bothered to light a fire in the hearth tonight. The heat he and Jane conjured together was more than enough to drive away the chill of the air. Now, he wished he had. Something about the haze drifting down the darkened hallway made him feel ill at ease. Imagining Jane wading through the mist on her lonely trek heightened the feeling into something close to dread.

Jane laughed at his worry about her solitary walk from the cottage to the big house's back door. On nights like this one, when the fog crept off the river and crept through the trees thicker than the typical morning mist, even Peter would have hesitated to wade through it. There was always something to trip over hidden on the ground. There was always something to be wary of when the path at his feet disappeared. The sound of the world around him changed. Direction became less certain. Common sense said that nights like this were best spent inside if he didn't need to venture out. Not his Jane, she would go out just to dance in the clouds. She was a force of nature all on her own. She scoffed at his warnings to be careful just as she brushed off his worry about the reaction everyone would have if they found out the truth of what had been going on between them.

Still, Peter did what he always did after the woman who held his heart in the palm of her hand gained enough distance from the cottage. He found his torch and slid his boots on. Throwing a jacket over his bare chest, he wandered out of his cottage door into the night to ensure she got home safely. If he were somehow discovered, he could always say that he was checking the pheasants or had heard a disturbance and gone out to investigate. No one would ask further unless it was to offer help. Peter's guilt would eat at him but there was nothing new there since he and Jane had begun their affair. Guilt was the price he paid for loving her. If it was all that was asked of him for the privilege of living in her dream world, he would count himself a very lucky man.

CHAPTER

FOUR

Adington Present Day

"Are we sure this is what we want?" Jay, one muscular arm curled lovingly around his wife's shoulders, the other ending in a loose fist in his pocket where he jingled a handful of change, asked. "It's a big move and far more land than we ever considered in the plan."

Laura, her jade green eyes searching the cottage with its beautiful front garden and the deep wood threaded with Footpaths behind it as if sure some secret hid just outside her peripheral vision, nodded. Jay was right, leaving the city to move to a cottage on the outskirts of a village that barely stretched wide enough to compare to the street they lived on would be a big change. The land that came with the stone house promised far more work than they had discussed while making their original plan. On the surface, a couple in their forties and used to the conveniences of busy streets and all that came with them should be more than a little intimidated. Instead, Laura felt drawn to Adington and the well-kept cottage currently being discussed so strongly that there was no denying it. This was home. It didn't matter to her that her life until less than a month ago had been spent without ever knowing it existed. Now that she was here, she knew this was where she and Jay belonged.

"Laura?" Jay bumped her when she didn't answer.

"Sorry," she turned a brilliant smile up to him. A warm, summer breeze trailed through her dark hair like a caress. "I was imagining what it will look like next year after we make it our home. So, yes, I'm sure. It's perfect, Jay, simply perfect. The timing, too, I know it sounds silly, but it feels like this cottage has been waiting for us."

Just then a shadow passed the window inside the cottage, "Jay, did you see that" "Who the ..." Jays words trailed off as the figure passed the upstairs window again. At that, Jay rushed through the cottage door and up the stairs. "No one here" he shouted down from the window. Laura lifted her arms and shrugged her shoulders. As Jay locked the door to the cottage, they realised it was probably the reflection of the trees in the window. "Just the way the light changes as it flickers through the branches, we will have to get used to living surrounded by nature" Laura beamed with her contagious smile. "Blimey that had my heart in my mouth there for a second" Jay was half laughing as he spoke. As they turned to walk down the path they heard dogs barking "Ow, sounds like some playmates for Harvey, people must use the footpaths at the back of the cottage" Laura said. "Odd as the whole area back there seems so overgrown but I guess we haven't explored it all yet" Jay put his arm around his beautiful wife and brought her close. They stopped and turned for one last look at Keepers Cottage before they had to go.

"WHAT WILL you do with yourself while I am off at the school in Keterton convincing my students that history is far more interesting than their textbook may imply?" It wasn't that Jay wanted to talk Laura out of leaving the city behind. He was more than ready for a slower pace and a closer-knit community. Adington offered that. Keterton, where the headmaster of the secondary school was waiting for him to sign on as a history teacher, was a short drive away. The cottage was in good repair. The land was well-kept. The asking price was well within their means. Still, something about the place made him uneasy now that they stood in front of it. An apartment in Keterton might be a good idea until they were more used to the area and got to know their neighbours. Leaving the woman he loved most in this world on her own all day in a strange place felt wrong.

"Silly man," Laura laughed and nestled against him. "When have I ever had trouble occupying my time? Besides, the plan we put together grows as soon as we sign a bit of paperwork. Instead of confining my design efforts to window box gardens and small plantings that add curb appeal, this cottage offers me the opportunity to show what my green fingers are capable of. Not only that, but I can build the loveliest greenhouse. There is plenty of room on the sunny side of the cottage. Not one of those boxy things the stores sell these days. I want to design a work of art that looks like it has been in place since the whole area was one big estate. Between all of that and the small changes we should make inside next spring, I will barely have time to notice you aren't home. Unless I run into some heavy lifting, of course. Or any time I need a second set of hands to get the video just right. Then, I will miss you to pieces."

"It sounds like we are exchanging our hard-earned savings to create a jade-eyed monster that plans to cover the world in flowers," Jay laughed as the tension he had felt all day slid away. Whatever doubts still lingered at the edges of his mind, Laura's contentment wasn't one of them.

"Now you. Are you sure? We both know that moving here means giving up any of my current clients who aren't willing to work with me remotely." This was one of the only sticking points for Laura. Her landscaping design firm might be tiny, but it helped keep the bills paid and allowed her and Jay to put away the money they had so far. That was the same money that would disappear as soon as they purchased the cottage. "If the video series doesn't draw in new clients, our plan isn't going to work."

"You have two years to make sure it does," Jay reminded her. "I can't see you failing with your mind so set on growing the business. If you ask me, you are going to be lucky if you aren't swamped with new clients long before you are finished transforming our cottage. We will have to live our lives in disarray because so many people will want your time and artist's eye. You know what they say about the cobbler's wife going barefoot. We will be living in a flowerless wasteland."

"Always the optimist," Laura got up on tip-toe and pulled Jay's face down for a kiss. "Just remember that when everything looks like a disaster because I'm trapped in the office with a deadline hanging over me and you can't find your belt because it got buried under one box of supplies or another."

"It wouldn't be the first time," Jay scooped her up into his arms. His Laura was a force of nature in her own right. She had turned her love of all growing things into a thriving business in the heart of a city with barely any room for green things. Now that they were taking a much-needed step closer to nature itself, he couldn't wait to see what his beautiful wife could do. If that meant hunting through a bit of chaos to find what he needed now and again, so be it. "Let's call the estate agent and see if we can buy the cottage, the weather looks right for a new adventure."

. . .

8 WEEKS later Jay and Laura arrived at Adington Inn, where they were staying for the night, as in the morning they would pick up the keys to "Keepers Cottage", their new home. Christine, the sweet-natured woman who ran the inn with an efficiency that bordered on precognition, recommended Kelse's pub, "The Hare" for both dinner and a cele-bratory drink before Laura even thought to ask.

They set out on the short walk to the pub, the evening sun was low and lit the river; it glinted and for a second as the sun hit her eyes, she saw a young man walking two large black dogs the other side of the river, he was waving and smiling at her, Laura waved back. "Everyone is so friendly here," Laura sighed happily "Can't wait to bring Harvey here, I hope he's behaving at the dog sitters house. The river walk will be an endless fascination to a terrier who has spent his entire life with only a dog park to romp in. I can't even imagine how long it will take him to get tired of the Footpaths."

"We will pick him up and bring him tomorrow, it's so great we have a dog sitter in the village who he seems to love already," Jay twined his fingers with hers as they walked. This was exactly what he needed. Fresh early evening air carried the sound of the river swishing against its banks, the birds were chattering wildly and his darling wife's excitement as she took it all in only made the moment better. "Then, you'll be telling me all about how he slipped his collar to chase rabbits and pester foxes."

"He will be too tired for that with a morning jog round the lake and paths through the woods after you leave for work," Laura laughed. "He'll sleep all day while I get things done. Then we'll take a more sedate stroll along the river walk to the village where we will meet you at the pub for a pint before we all head back home. Any rabbits, foxes, or pheasants - because I saw a small flock of those out back while we were giving our last-minute doubts time to settle this morning- and any of our wild neighbours that don't feel like having the attention of our furry boy will just have to do their best to avoid tempting him into a game of chase."

"He most likely wouldn't have any idea of what to do if he caught them, anyway," Jay laughed. "That rubber ball of his proves challenging enough most days."

WHEN THEY REACHED THE PUB, Jay held the door open and ushered her inside. He could see the dream Laura had for their life here as clear as day. He gave the people of Adington a week before they realized that he and his darling wife had bought the cottage.

"You must be the couple that just bought old Pete Marsh's cottage behind the inn," the bartender said as Jay and Laura found a seat.

"Peter Marsh was barely out of short pants when he was sent off to the hereafter," a thin man with eyes as grey as his hair said from two stools down.

"Finish your pint, Jim. You know that daughter of yours likes you home before she gets the kids in bed," the bartender said, levelling a warning look. He turned back to Jay and Laura. "Don't mind Jim. Oh, and don't mind the speed at which the village heard about its newest members. I'm Martin Kelse, not to be confused with my great grandfather who was also Martin and originally opened this pub back in the day."

"Jay and Laura," Jay held out a hand and was met with a solid handshake. "Nice to meet you, that's why it's known as Kelse's pub then. I have to say, we weren't expecting news to travel quite so fast."

"You'll get used to it," Martin laughed. "Privacy is sacred around here so long as you understand that it only extends as far as your closed curtains. As soon as the for-sale sign went up on the cottage it became the main conversation around the here. The place has been empty longer than some of us have been alive. It's nice to know it's going to be put to use again."

"Nice to meet you" Jim stretched out a hand, Just make sure you sweep the river fog out in the mornings if it reaches your door," Jim winked. "If any place around here is going to attract the spirits wandering in, it's the keeper's cottage."

"We talked about this, Jim." Martin rolled his eyes. "Don't pay him any mind. What can I get for you this evening?"

"Ah no Martin, it's important to keep to the traditions," Jim nodded as he stared into his pint. "No sense in courting disaster by letting them slip away."

"How about you slip on back home," Martin said collecting Jim's glass when the old man drained it. "There's no sense in trying to scare off our new friends before the ink on their contract is even dry, now is there?"

"I hear you, Martin." Jim stood up and laid some money on the counter. "No doubt see you around" he nodded to Laura and Jay as he left.

"What was that all about?" Laura could barely

hold in her giggle until the door closed behind the old man and Jay placed their order.

"It's an old Adington superstition," Martin said. "Every foggy morning started with sweeping the mist back out the front door so spirits wouldn't linger. I suppose every village has its ghost stories. Don't let ours give you too many goosebumps. Enjoy a pint on the house as my welcome while you wait for your food. We'll have music this evening if you want to meet your new neighbours."

"Maybe once we're in." Laura smiled. "The next few days are going to be busy, and I think tonight I need my sleep, the removal men turn up in the morning."

"Ah! Well, that will be busy for you, you are, of course, always welcome," Martin assured them both. "There isn't always music but the crowd is friendly. We'll make you feel right at home before you can blink an eye."

Two days later, after the movers finished stacking boxes and fitting their furniture through the cottage door, ghosts were the last thing on Laura's mind. She was too busy helping Jay try to hunt down an icy draft coming from their bedroom. How it was so cold was a mystery, considering the warm sun beating down outside.

"Maybe we should just swap out the bedroom and the office," she suggested. "I won't be in here much at the start and the other room is just as big. Besides, it's closer to the kitchen so stumbling out to make coffee will be easier."

"That will work for now," Jay sighed. His normal, jovial nature had taken a hit almost as soon as he walked through the cottage door. Now he had an ache at his temples and his stomach churned miserably. "It's just one more thing on the list. For all that this cottage looks like it was cared for, I don't understand how the surveyor could have missed so many problems."

"I haven't noticed nearly as many as you have," Laura walked over to wrap her arms around his solid chest. "Are you sure you slept well last night?"

"I slept fine," Jay grumbled. "Maybe the cottage just likes you more and isn't showing you its ugly side."

"Could be," Laura poked him playfully in the shoulder. "I do seem rather more likable today than you, after all. Who could blame it?"

"Point taken," Jay wrapped his arms around her and kissed the top of her head. "Consider my bad mood a thing of the past. Let's team up on the newly relocated bedroom so there is some hope that we can sleep on our own pillows tonight. I will go and collect Harvey from the dog sitter, now we are a bit straighter."

"Off you go, then," Laura gave him a nudge toward the door. "If you want a little extra head-clearing time, feel free to pick up dinner while you are out. Then, we won't be forced to cobble something together out of the few groceries I have in one of those boxes piled on the counter."

"Consider it done," Jay tipped her chin up with a finger and gave her a lingering kiss. He hoped she couldn't see how disheartened he felt now that they were moving in. Her enthusiasm over the cottage was having trouble cutting through the murky exhaustion that bogged him down almost as soon as the movers drove off. "Are you sure you'll be alright if I leave you to it that long?"

"Course I'll be fine" Laura shook her head. "Go get some air. By the time you get back, a great number of these boxes may be out of the way and we will both be able to start seeing our new home taking shape around us."

Maybe that was the problem, Jay decided as he made his way back toward the river. There was so much to do in the cottage, much more than he had realized. Now that he was away from it all, his mood was already lifting.

He picked up Harvey and then took his time on the walk to the village pub. A couple of their new neighbours stopped to chat. More waved. The only one who didn't acknowledge him in some way was a youngish man walking two black labs beside the water. Jay shrugged it off. The man looked like he was lost in thought, and the dogs were too busy snuffling at the ground to notice anything else. Besides, Harvey was pulling at the leash and looking nervous with all the new attention. There would be time to get to know everyone after the boxes disappeared and order was restored in their new home.

"Now for you," Laura said to the kitchen once she was alone. She liked talking to the space she worked in. It might seem silly to someone who didn't know her but something about the one-sided conversations always made her understand what needed to be done better. "Don't take this wrong, but you have been alone for far too long. You need a woman's touch. Nothing drastic, mind you. Just a few changes to lighten things up and drive out some of your old shadows. What do you think?"

Almost as if the cottage agreed, the kitchen light flickered.

"That better not be the wiring," Laura sighed. She measured out coffee and filled the pot as she talked her way through her ideas for the kitchen. "Jay is already at his wit's end. I can tell. If it's just the bulb needing a replacement, that would be wonderful. Changing out the fixture is acceptable although I would much rather wait until after the rest is finished. Some new tiles for the backsplash after I strip the old varnish off of the cupboards and refinish them with a lighter stain. The butcher block counter can be sanded and resealed so nothing major there. The same for all of the floors, I think. I can add a centre Island, there is enough space for that. And just think how wonderful it will be when we have friends over."

The coffee maker began gurgling. Laura turned, confused. She was sure she hadn't turned it on. Jay wouldn't be back for a while and she wanted to offer him a fresh cup when he arrived.

"Wow, I must really be distracted," Laura shrugged and poured herself a cup once the pot was full. No doubt the extra caffeine would clear her head and make scrubbing the cupboards go faster. She raised a toast to the kitchen. "Here is to new beginnings."

The light flickered again, and Laura raised an

eyebrow at it. Maybe installing a new fixture first would be a smarter idea. The ceiling could use a coat of nice, bright white while she was at it. Starting at the top and working her way down made sense. For now, a good cleaning would have to do. She suddenly felt an icy chill wind its way around her legs and the hairs on the back of her neck stood on end. It was like someone had just walked in and was stood behind her. She spun around but there was no one there. Then a strange odour filled the air, and it was strong enough to override the deep richness of the coffee. The nearest thing she could liken it to was the scent of spent fireworks. Laura turned to open the kitchen window and she saw him. Well, more a shadow moving away from the cottage. Her knees buckled and she sat with a bump to the floor. She pulled her knees in close and held them tight. "Shit, that was strange" She felt her breathing steady now and the smell was gone. Just the smell of fresh coffee lingered in the air. As she stood up, she peered over the kitchen top, just able to see a glimpse out of the window. A beautiful sunny day, not a cloud in the sky. She sighed a huge breath out.

"Oh, don't tell me you have issues with the place already, Harvey," Jay gave the terrier's leash a gentle tug when he reached the cottage an hour later.

Harvey, nose up and sniffing the air with a high-pitched whine, didn't budge. "You haven't even been inside yet. Come on. Dinner will get cold and I'll bet your bed is already waiting for you inside."

Time away from his new home had done Jay a world of good. He felt energized. The headache with its accompanying hint of heartburn was gone. By the time he and Harvey walked back from the village, Jay was ready for a hearty meal, and an evening of shifting furniture around. After that, he fully intended to make the woman he had married two decades ago believe it was their wedding night all over again.

"Laura, love, call your dog. I've got an armload of fish and chips and he seems to believe that ten feet from his new front door is quite close enough. I think it's a trick. His nose has been twitching toward the bags since we left the pub. If I try to pick him up, he's going to make sure everything lands on the ground where he can reach it." The cottage was pretty in the late afternoon light. Jay would give it that. What he wouldn't give it was credit for having had a solid inspection before they bought it. If his suspicions were correct, he and Laura were going to find more than just a draft that needed to be sealed up by the end of their renovation. He gave Harvey's lead another tug when Laura didn't answer. The terrier obliged by inching toward the front door with his tail tucked between his legs and his ears back. "Harvey, really! Pull yourself together and act like the brave dog you believe you are anytime a package arrives. This is embarrassing."

Just as quickly as the Harvey started acting strangely, he perked up, shook off whatever had bothered him, and raced to the door nearly throwing Jay off balance.

"The door's stuck again, Laura," Jay banged on the solid wood with his elbow. "And Harvey has the leash wrapped at least three times around my ankles. Do us a favour and open up."

"What do you mean the door's stuck?" Laura asked swinging it open effortlessly. "Ah, food! I'm starving."

She took the bags and left Jay to untangle himself on the threshold. Harvey, excited now that his initial trepidation was gone, didn't make the job any easier.

"Oh no you don't," catching the door as a breeze tried to shut it in his face, Jay finally gave up and unclipped Harvey's collar from the leash. The terrier raced into the house with his nose working overtime to take in all the new scents. "I picked up a sanding block for you while I was out. We'll be done with this sticking business in no time."

"You look like that walk did you good," Laura reached up and caressed Jay's' cheek. "Your colour is back and your eyes aren't nearly as squinty."

"It was all the fresh air," Jay looked around at the progress Laura had made while he was gone. Even with so much left to do, the cottage was already starting to feel like home. "Speaking of which. I see you opened some windows."

"It took a bit of doing," Laura smiled as she looked around. "Between the boxes and someone's overly generous use of paint on the trim, I had a time of it. There was this odd smell. It reminded me of that time we went to see the fireworks and the smoke got caught in the drizzle that was coming down. Not that strong. Just the same type of scent. I'm sure it's coming from one of the boxes but I haven't been able to find it yet."

"Maybe that's what had Harvey skittish outside. I don't smell anything now, but his nose is far better than mine." The kitchen light flickered once drawing his attention. "Has that happened before?"

"Once just after you left," Laura admitted with a cringe. "I checked the fixture and the switch and didn't see any cause for alarm. I think it's just a faulty bulb. If I had extra, I would have already replaced it."

"I'll turn it off for now" Jay hung up Harvey's leash by the door. His headache was coming back. "We can manage without the kitchen light tonight and I'll give the wiring a good going over tomorrow. It could very well be the source of the smell too"

"We'll eat as soon as you come back," Laura called after him. "I've got a lovely table for two set up in front of the fireplace. It will be just like our first meal in that tiny little apartment we moved into after our wedding."

By the time they made it to bed that night, both Jay and Laura were so tired their heads barely touched the pillows before they sank into sleep. Jay's dreams were chaotic. Shadows within shadows wound through the maze of those subconscious manifestations. He ran with Laura laughing beneath the sun one minute. The next, mist that tasted like gunpowder engulfed them and his hands were coated in blood.

Jay sat bolt upright in the bed with sweat pouring off him. His heart hammered painfully behind his ribcage. The nightmare echoed through his body with a force that made his hands shake even as it faded. Beside him, Laura murmured something and curled closer. Her hand found his as she slept on. Her long, slender fingers wrapped like a lifeline around his palm. Carefully, so he would not wake her, Jay lifted her hand to his lips and kissed the soft skin at her wrist. Laura always knew when he needed her. Even in sleep, she somehow sensed his unease and made the vital connection that brought him peace.

He lay thinking how silent it was, peaceful, so why did he feel so uneasy? Then he heard them, distinct footsteps and the floorboards creaking just beyond the bedroom door, Jay's froze, lifting his head so he could hear better. Very, very slowly, the door to the bedroom creaked open. If someone was there, Harvey would have been crazy barking. Then silence again. Tucking Laura's hand gently back against her pillow, he slipped from their bed and turned the phone torch on. Harvey cocked his head and stared at the door from his moonlit spot nestled against the back of Laura's knees. The terrier's nose was up, sniffing the air again. He sneezed once and then settled back down with his head on his paws, but his eyes still trained on the door.

"What is it, boy?" Jay asked in a whisper. The cottage was totally quiet, not even the hum of the refrigerator filled the void as Jay's ears strained in the deafening quiet.

Feeling foolish, Jay looked back at his sleeping wife as he stood naked, phone in hand, and filled with the same unnamed dread that the darkness had conjured in him as a child. Logic told him that the sound of the floorboards was nothing more than a temperature shift. The ominous weight of the moment was just the last lingering remnants of his nightmare. There was nothing in the cottage that could harm Laura. And yet, he needed to check. There would be no getting back to sleep until he did.

"Stay," he ordered Harvey when the dog perked up again.

Nothing was amiss. Not in the bedroom, or among the maze of boxes still taking up the bulk of the space in the lounge

The office was a jumble of hastily relocated belongings. Aside from a drip of water hanging on the shower head, the bathroom was just as he left it after scrubbing off the day. The only small thing out of place anywhere was Laura's coffee mug in the sink while his cup remained on the counter. For some reason, that detail triggered the unease inside him. Those mugs were nearly as inseparable as he and Laura. They sat together when they weren't in use whether that was beside the coffee maker or in the sink. To see them apart in the darkness felt wrong.

Jay sensed that he was being watched and swung the light around quickly. As it glinted off the window he saw a face, looking right at him. A young, haunted face with sunken dark eyes.... It was gone almost before his brain went into full alert. Racing to the door, Jay wrenched it open and swept the garden with his light. No one was there. Not even a footprint in the night-damp grass lent credence to the idea that some stranger had invaded the sanctity of his home.

"You are a grown man, Jay. Stop being ridiculous," he told himself before swearing softly. "Not only a grown man but a naked one standing outside looking for an intruder like a lunatic." He was seeing things, he was half asleep, tired. His mind was playing tricks on him. Was it his own reflection?

The sound of the door slamming behind him, caused him to literally yell out in fear. He ran at the door "NO NO NO! Fuck it!" He could hear Harvey barking, running around inside. Moments later he hears Laura calling him. "I'm outside, let me in".

The door opened. The explanation for him being the other side of it naked was tricky. He didn't want to scare her so he said he couldn't sleep and thought he would go out and look at the stars. He could tell she didn't really believe him but didn't question further.

A box of Laura's chamomile tea rested in the box of groceries still waiting to be put in the cupboard. Normally, Jay hated the stuff. Tonight, he made an exception and when Laura handed it to him, he drank it down gratefully. He wasn't going to sleep though; his mind was racing. He knew what he had seen and heard, no matter how much he told himself otherwise.

CHAPTER

FIVE

954

"Everything is in order for the start of the festival tomorrow?" John Noble greeted his daughters at breakfast with a kiss to the top of their heads just as he had done every morning for as long as Jane could remember.

"We were just sorting a spot for a last-minute vendor," Jane pointed out an option for Sarah as she spoke. "Their prior engagement was rescheduled, and they would be a good addition."

"They make honey," Sarah tilted her head to consider the location.

"I'm afraid I need to pull Jane away," John said. Jane gave him a quizzical look and found her father smiling wider than usual. At her raised eyebrow, that smile increased even more. "We have guests arriving. William and Clara Fields from one of our neighbouring estates will be joining us through the week of the festival along with their son Richard. We are considering growing the event next year to include their land. I have promised that Jane will ensure that Richard has a wonderful time while we hash out some of the details."

"Why me?" Jane had a sickening suspicion based on the triumphant gleam in her father's eye. There was a secret there. One that he was simply bursting to share.

"The two of you are of an age," John sounded far too casual about the statement for his eldest daughter's liking. "Who better to show him around the festivities and introduce him?"

"Sarah," Jane suggested instantly. "No one cringes when she walks toward them. Besides, I have my hands far too full to play hostess. You did give me the job of ensuring that the event runs smoothly, Father. I can't do that and take a personal interest in one guest's experience at the same time."

"Sarah can manage the event from here," John turned to his youngest daughter. "Can't you, my dear?"

"Of course," Sarah agreed although she gave

Jane a worried look. "Jane has done a wonderful job of laying the groundwork. If you need her elsewhere, I am sure that I can manage."

"It's settled, then!" John lifted his cup of tea and saluted Sarah with his toast. "Now, Jane, I know this is a somewhat spur-of-the-moment change to your schedule. I assure you that I have the utmost faith in your ability to adapt. To help, I have prepared a list of activities I believe Richard might enjoy that will also allow him the opportunity to see our home in its best light. Cooperation with our neighbours will help us all thrive. I am confident that you are the very person most able to point out what we have to offer to any future agreements. I expect you to take this opportunity to shine seriously. None of your usual shenanigans. None of those horrible denim trousers. We want our guests to see that even in times of frivolity, our estate, and the village of Adington understand refinement. The Fields have just returned to the area after far too many years abroad. We want them to feel welcome."

Jane took the list with a sinking feeling in the pit of her stomach. There was only one reason that her father would have gone to this much trouble. If she remembered correctly, Richard had been sent off to boarding school while his parents were away on business. That was years ago. The chances were good that he hadn't been apprised of the problematic nature of the eldest Noble daughter. There was a far better chance that John Noble was playing matchmaker than trusting her to make a good business connection through hard work and knowledge of the land.

"No," Jane whispered. She wasn't about to voice her suspicions aloud, but she might still be able to talk some sense into the man. She cleared her throat to dislodge the lump of fear forming there. "Father, please reconsider having Sarah handle this and leaving me to oversee the festival. Even on my best day, we all know that I am liable to make a mess of things in this type of situation."

"Nonsense," John waved her concerns away with his toast. "You'll do fine. Remember, I have nothing but faith in you."

With one final overly excited grin, he popped the last bite of his breakfast into his mouth, drained his cup, and brushed the crumbs from his fingers. Then, humming a jaunty tune, he was gone.

"Jane?" Sarah asked in a tone that implied she might be speaking to a particularly unruly mental patient. "Are you alright?"

Jane snapped her mouth closed and picked up

the itinerary from the floor where it had slipped through her fingers. Alright? Absolutely not! She had gone to sleep with the velvety touch of her lover still tingling on her skin and woken to a nightmare in which her father was foisting her off on the neighbour's son.

"He's trying to marry me off," The words came out more like a whimper than anything else. She was much more comfortable with anger. "That's the only explanation for this sudden change of plans. He believes that this Richard is still fresh enough to our circle that my reputation as a troublemaker can't have reached him yet. Did you see the way he smiled? He never smiles like that when something involves me."

"I'm sure he is just allowing you to prove the rumours about you wrong, Jane," Sarah had her diplomatic face on. Jane wanted to shake her. "Sometimes a fresh start with a new face is just the thing to rectify past mistakes. Besides, how bad could it be? A week in the company of a man who hasn't had time to become a nuisance to you can't be a terrible way to spend your time. Plus, I hear he is rather good-looking. Look on the bright side, Jane. Stop expecting the worst out of everyone. Especially stop expecting it from yourself."

"I'm not expecting the worst from myself," Jane snapped. "Nor am I expecting it from someone I haven't even met. It isn't my expectations that are the problem here. I wish you, at least, could see that."

She wasn't hungry anymore. Leaving her half-eaten breakfast behind, Jane stormed out of the dining room as tears gathered along her lashes. She needed Peter. If anyone in the world could save her from what she felt sure was unfolding, it was him. She could convince him to run away. She knew she could. They could leave tonight. Before then, if she found a way to slip past her father and his guests without being noticed. It didn't matter where they went. As long as Peter was by her side, her world would be perfect.

"I've laid out your dress, Miss," the stranger standing in her room said as soon as Jane threw the door open.

"Who are you?" Jane took in the sedate uniform as a ball of dread took shape in the pit of her stomach.

"My name is Eleanor. Your father hired me to look after your personal needs through the week. I am to see to your hair and clothing as well as helping you maintain your schedule." She looked pleasant enough although her back was ramrod straight and there was an undercurrent to her introduction that gave Jane the impression that she was used to dealing with unruly girls. "If you will sit down, we can begin. Your guests will arrive within the hour. We wouldn't want you to be late."

"We don't have servants here," Jane said incredulously. "Aside from the kitchen staff but that's different. We don't have maids."

"You do this week," Eleanor said pleasantly. "Your father assures me that my presence will help you a great deal."

"Does Sarah have a maid as well?" Jane inched backward toward the door.

"Of course," Eleanor smiled. "Think of my presence as a treat. I've been given the room right across the hall along with your itinerary. Both should help the week go smoothly with so many constraints on your time."

Eleanor had the nerve to take Jane by the arm and guide her to the chair in front of her vanity. This was never going to do. Jane stood no chance of escaping with the woman so focused on her. It was as if she was thrown back in time to the days of having a nanny overseeing her every move.

"Now, I believe that the lovely forest green dress

that was delivered along with an array of other options this morning will do beautifully for your initial greeting and introductions. Once this afternoon's luncheon concludes, you can change into riding pants and a white turtleneck sweater with this lovely navy jacket for a guided tour of the grounds. This evening's dinner will be late, so the more formal copper gown seems appropriate. I do wish your hair was a bit longer. That dress would be set off all the more by an updo. I'll have to see what ornamentation I can find and possibly add some curls." Eleanor rattled on as Jane stared into the mirror, wishing she could disappear entirely. "Just some light makeup to enhance your fine bone structure, I think. Nothing too bright or it will look garish on you. You are truly lovely, my dear. Not all women are blessed with a face pretty enough to be seen without lipstick."

Her father had thought of everything. New clothes, new riding boots, new baubles and the stranger currently tipping Jane's chin this way and that to ensure that they were all put to use. It was crushing. Jane doubted she would recognize herself when she left the room. She shivered at the thought.

The shock alone kept Jane from putting up a fight as Eleanor began performing her duties. All she could do was agree with everything the woman said to try to shorten the duration of this new insult to her very being. Yes, the dress was lovely. Of course, the small flip of her hair at each cheek was perfect for the day. The new pumps were, indeed, as comfortable as they looked. All the while, Jane was screaming inside.

When she was finally set free, she could barely stomach a glance in the mirror. The woman she saw there was someone else entirely.

"So, this is who my father wants me to be," Jane nearly laughed. "I'm sure he'll be tickled pink to see his new daughter. She looks so much more upstanding and refined than the one he had."

Eleanor had the decency not to comment. Instead, she ushered Jane out the door just in time to join the rest of the family in the foyer as their guests arrived.

"You look lovely, my dears," John Noble's eyes twinkled at the sight of his daughters. His gaze lingered longer on Jane. It wasn't her imagination that he looked relieved by what he saw. "Jane, do manage a smile if you would. We are not at a funeral."

"Of course, Father," Jane did her best to tip her lips enough to make him happy. She had to find a way out. If she could reach Peter, she would convince him to take her away from this nightmare. The only way to do that was to play along until the right moment presented itself.

Sarah gave her a wary look but quickly composed herself as their father motioned for the doors to be opened.

Outside, a large car pulled up. A couple got out. Once they stepped away from the doors, their son followed. He was pleasant to look at, Jane would give him that. His smile was easy as he extended his hand when introduced. His laugh was genuine if sedate as his father made some affable joke at his expense. Overall, there was nothing to dislike in Richard Fields much to Jane's dismay. She had hoped he would be a toad of a man with the manners of a rabid squirrel. Instead, she had to hate him based solely on the machinations she was now even more sure were in play around them.

"You are much quieter than I was led to believe," Richard said hours later as they rode along the far boundary of John Noble's land. "I was under the impression that you were a bit outspoken."

"I'm just a little tired today," Jane gave him a small smile. None of this was Richard's fault. He was a pawn in this game as much as she was.

While she could not tell him the full truth, she could at least offer a pleasant lie. "I put a lot of my time and energy into planning the festival this year. I thought I would be seeing it through. Father only told me this morning that my plans had changed. I'm having a hard time switching gears."

"Because you are now expected to set that aside and play nursemaid to a grown man," Richard laughed without humour. "I understand. I thought I was coming along so I could offer my opinions on growing the festival and our estate in general, not to take a vacation with the lovely daughter of my host as my tour guide."

"We could always throw the itinerary out the window and reinsert ourselves into our proper roles," Jane raised an eyebrow in question.

"Or, we could let them struggle through without us, spend the week doing as we please, and enjoy ourselves far more than their list of activities will allow." Richard circled his horse to take up a position closer to her. "Call it a compromise. We can start by turning this stately walk around the estate into a race and go from there."

"Compromise," Jane threw her head back and laughed. "You really need to spend some time with my sister, Sarah. The two of you would get along famously."

"Now that I live so close, I'm sure that I will have plenty of time to get to know everyone. Adington is lovely but it will never overwhelm a man with options on a Saturday night. Neither will the other villages within an easy drive." Richard looked out over the land. From where they stood, they could see the sprawling lands of both the Noble and the Fields estates.

"Does that bother you?" Jane found herself genuinely curious. "Being in the country instead of the city, I mean."

"Not at all." Richard's smile was relaxed when he turned it to her. "I had my fill of big city life while I was abroad. It was nice for a time but building up the family lands has always been my dream. It isn't as if the estate will be a prison. If I feel the need for Paris or London or anywhere in the world for that matter, I can always travel. This is home. I may not have spent much time here until now, but this is where I want to build my future." He paused and scanned the tall grass once more. "How do you feel about sheep?"

"I enjoy wearing the sweaters their wool makes and a good leg of lamb on the table. Beyond that, they are far too docile for my liking." Jane shrugged. "Why do you ask?"

"My parents may have their hearts set on event planning as a retirement vocation but my interests in the family estate have a broader range. It's nice to have a second opinion from someone I'm told understands the land itself," Peter stretched his arm out to sweep across the horizon. "Sheep might be a good option."

"It sounds like you've been told quite a bit about me," the tickle of dread Jane had felt skipping up her spine all day amplified as she tried to make light of her accusation.

"Enough to know that you aren't yourself at the moment unless I was lied to," Richard flashed a dazzling smile at her. "Don't worry. I always look for the best possible meaning of any euphemism being used to describe someone. You are welcome to throw caution to the wind and just be yourself, Jane. Unless, of course, *wilful* was a nice way of saying that you throw knives at your dinner guests if they say the wrong thing in which case I would appreciate some warning so I can duck."

"I can't say that I have ever let my frustrations out in quite that way," Jane laughed. She had to admit that if she was forced to spend the week with a stranger, Richard Fields was a far better option than she could have been handed. "Some things I've said in the past might be considered just as sharp, and there was that one time when I may have kicked a rock after one of the gentlemen on a stalking expedition spooked my deer just as I was about to take a shot. I didn't mean for it to hit his shin, so it shouldn't be counted as anything more than an accident."

"And there she is," Richard grinned and held out his hand. "It is a pleasure to meet you, Jane Noble."

Jane shook his hand. There was no spark, not like when Peter touched her. Instead, it was as if Richard was a long-lost friend. She smiled as the persistently nagging ball of unnameable fear nestled in her stomach settled down to something more manageable.

"Did you mention a race earlier?" Just the thought of giving her horse his head and letting the wind whip around her as he ran made Jane feel free for the first time since breakfast.

"I did." Richard checked his watch. "And we have just enough time for me to win before we are due for dinner. Shall we make it more interesting with a bet?"

"First one back to the fence before the barn gets

to decide how to alter tomorrow's planned excursions?" Jane offered.

"I like how you think," Richard agreed. "Ready? Set. Go!"

Jane's feeling of divine freedom was short-lived. As soon as she entered the house, she was whisked away to prepare for the drudgery of a formal meal. Eleanor admonished her for the light sheen of sweat Jane had worked up during the race, the redness in her cheeks, and the state of her hair. She ordered Jane into a bath, after which the maid tutted at her more about being ladylike as she arranged her hair and helped her into her dress.

Then it was off to make small talk, which Jane loathed doing. The Fields were nice enough but there was little substance to the conversation overall. The meal was enjoyable but, it too, felt as if the courses were on a tight schedule, giving no one time to linger over what was on their plates. The whole evening felt far too contrived to be comfortable.

By the time the evening was finally over, Jane was exhausted from her efforts to be someone she wasn't just to please her father. Doing so was still her best option. If he felt he could trust her to do what was expected, perhaps he would relax enough for her to escape once and for all.

"Close that window!" Eleanor demanded just as Jane thought she was done with the woman for the night. "You'll catch your death."

"I just needed some air, Eleanor," Jane breathed in the chilly night noting that there would be a thick layer of fog once again.

For the first time since she was a child, Jane entertained the old stories her nanny would tell her to keep her and Sarah in their beds. Jane had never let on that the stories of ghosts wandering in the misty blanket creeping over the ground thrilled rather than scared her. She would lie beneath the covers imagining that just outside her window the spirits of those who had once walked this earth as flesh and bone were dancing beneath the light of the moon. Who was to say that they were lost souls? In Jane's mind, she saw no fiends out to steal her away in the night. If the departed now clothed themselves in the natural world, it could only be because they loved the land so dearly. There was no fear to be found there when her own soul understood that love so well.

"And now that you have, you'll close the window," Eleanor directed in her best nanny voice. "And you will see that it stays closed. You have an early morning to wake up for and plenty to do with the day ahead. You need your rest. I've brought you some warm milk to help you sleep."

That was how the rest of the festive week went. Every second was taken up with something. There was no time to sneak off to see Peter who was constantly on her mind. There was barely time to breathe. Eleanor was like a guard dog, just waiting to herd Jane back where she belonged if she tried to slip from her room at night. During the day, Jane was lucky if she even caught a glimpse of her beloved Peter since very few of her father's plans put her and Richard in the festival itself. The few words she was able to exchange with Peter were stilted on both sides. They had to be. There were far too many eyes that might be on them. Jane finally had to resort to slipping him a note after showing Richard the pheasant pens at just the right time to catch Peter feeding the birds.

Let's run away together, the message said. *I will go wherever you choose. We can start fresh somewhere far from here. We can be free to be who we are and to love each other without fear. We can build a new life. Meet me in the clearing once the festival is over and we can leave this place. It is no longer my home. Your heart is. I love you, Peter. With all of my being, I love you.*

She slipped the unsigned note into the empty

bucket while Richard asked questions about the flock. Peter, bless his heart, made sure that it found its way into his pocket just as stealthily. Jane began counting the moments until her dream could come true.

"I was asked to come find you and Mr. Fields," Sally said with what was supposed to pass as a smile. Jane saw something completely different in the girl's eyes. Gears were turning behind them that raised goosebumps on Jane's arms. Had she seen the exchange? Jane had been so careful. Peter had, too. Surely, whatever calculations were going on in Sally's head were unrelated. Far too much depended on it. "You are needed back at the house."

"Is everything alright?" Jane's heart stuttered. She and Richard weren't scheduled for anything other than enjoying the festival right now.

"I'm sure it is," Richard interrupted. "I asked to speak to your father after breakfast. He said that he would send word when he had a moment. Perhaps we can take a picnic to the river for lunch afterward. There are some plans I would like to talk over with you."

Richard had been an unexpected bright spot throughout the week. In many ways, he felt like Jane's only friend in the whirlwind of her days.

Sarah was always busy elsewhere. Peter was inaccessible. Richard's willingness to let her be in the places that gave her the most peace was the only reason she was able to hold herself together instead of stepping over some line and embarrassing everyone with her words or actions. A picnic would satisfy her father's strange need to have her introduce Richard to the area yet let her be in a place where Eleanor wasn't watching every single move she made.

"A picnic sounds lovely," Jane agreed. While she would have much rather spent it with Peter, Richard at least tried to make their time together pleasant. The festival felt far too crowded, especially with Sally waiting to lead them back to the house as if they couldn't find their way, and Peter so close yet so out of reach beside the pheasant pens.

It wasn't until they were in the foyer that Jane realized how mistaken she had been. She should have never relaxed her guard. She should not have fallen for Richard's pleasant demeanour or the charming way that he always seemed willing to go along with her suggestions for the day.

Jane's heart sank as the man sank to one knee while their families looked on with bright smiles. She felt as cold as the marble floor beneath her feet and as trapped as one of the rabbits she caught in her snares.

"Jane Noble, I know we haven't known each other long but I feel that it might take me the rest of my life to truly understand the woman that you are. I would be honoured if you would give me that time. Will you marry me?" Richard looked so genuine in his proposal that it almost broke Jane's heart.

"No," Jane whispered. She cleared her throat and repeated her answer louder before adding, "Richard, you are a good man. You are beyond good. I know that. I also know that I will never love you how you deserve to be loved. I'm sorry. I'm so very sorry."

Richard shook his head. Getting to his feet, he cursed under his breath and gave her father a hard look before turning back to Jane. "No. You do not need to apologise, Jane. I misread the situation. My intentions are very real, however, I never would have asked you this quickly had I not believed you were as interested in that outcome as I am. Perhaps once we have known each other longer, my offer will be more appealing."

Jane turned and ran. Her heart beat so hard in her chest that she was afraid it might explode. Tears blinded her and only a lifetime's worth of memory carried her to her room.

"Jane Noble, you get down here this instant!" her father yelled after her. Then, in a far more placating tone, "I will see this sorted out, Richard. I'm sure the girl is just beside herself at the moment. She's excitable and prone to speaking before she thinks. Why doesn't everyone adjourn to the dining room for refreshments? It won't take long for Jane to come to her senses and see reason. She's a smart girl even if she isn't showing it at the moment. We'll join you once she's calmed down and put this unpleasantness behind us."

"Mr. Noble, may I have a word?" Jane's feet felt like lead as she heard Sally's voice float up the stairway. She sounded triumphant beneath the overly polite request.

Jane's heart pounded harder. She had to get away. She needed enough time to gather a few precious things from her room, then she would escape this house once and for all. She would find Peter. There was no reason to stay, and every reason to leave as quickly as possible.

It wasn't until she had stuffed a small bag full of the few things she felt she could not leave behind and tried to leave her room that Jane found it was locked from the outside. She tried the handle again to no avail. Finally, she balled up her fists and beat on the wood blocking her path to freedom.

"I have been instructed to see that you remain in your room until you have calmed down, Jane," Eleanor's stern voice said pleasantly through the thick wood. "Whatever the trouble is, I'm sure it can be handled far better with a clear head. Your father will be up shortly to speak with you. I suggest that you make the best use of your solitude by formulating an apology and coming up with a solution to rectify the turmoil you have caused."

Jane flew to the window and threw it open. She couldn't breathe. There was no escape from its height but at least there was cool air to battle the feverish panic coursing through her veins. She closed her eyes and breathed it in, willing her heart to slow and her mind to work. She would find a way to get to Peter. She had to. The life they were both meant for depended on it.

CHAPTER

SIX

Present day

By midmorning the next day, Laura was as ready for a break as Jay was. She hadn't slept well and the morning sun wasn't enough to lift an uneasy feeling she had. Judging by Jay's jumpiness, she knew he felt the same. Even Harvey was acting strangely. When he wasn't skirting wide around empty space with his tail tucked between his legs, he was planted on Jay and Laura's bed staring at the door. Even his favourite red ball was ignored in a far corner of the living room that the terrier refused to go near.

"Let's never put ourselves through a move again," Laura announced as she stretched her aching back. "My body doesn't like all of this lifting and scrubbing."

"Then you aren't going to like my idea at all," Jay turned an apologetic smile to her. He knew that what he was about to suggest wasn't going to sit well. Between his midnight search and the morning's nearly constant dodging of a draft so cold that he was surprised not to see frost coating the skirting boards, his mind was made up.

Laura turned to him with a raised eyebrow and a third mug of strong coffee in her hand. The look she gave him dared Jay to keep talking even as it threatened severe repercussions if he did.

"Not a move," Jay held both hands up warding off the formidable temper his beautiful wife rarely showed. "Just a pause in our settling in."

"Go on," Laura's tone suggested that she was prepared to let him dig a hole for himself but that she had no intention of helping him out of it once he reached the bottom.

"Let's go for lunch at the pub. We can talk about what I am proposing there. We both need a break from the cottage." He thought better of speaking about it so early in the day and got on with heaving boxes here and there.

As irrational as the thought made him feel, he

could do nothing to stop it. The place felt watchful, as if the stones themselves pressed closer to hear every word. Whatever scale it would use to measure them was weighted with a malevolent finger. Just as he was thinking about it, there was a bang on the wall of the bathroom. "You ok?" he shouted up.

"Yes, I'm ok," Laura sighed scooping her hair back from her face with both hands. "It's the pipes I think." Everything was getting to her today. All she wanted to do was curl up under the covers and go back to sleep. Maybe when she woke the next time, she would feel more like herself. Barring that, some fresh air and a break might at least give her the motivation she needed. "I don't know why this day feels so long already but it does. Maybe food will help me find my ambition again."

"I've been thinking," Jay said once they were settled in at one of the small tables. He desperately wanted a pint but had settled for something fizzy instead. He was already struggling for clear-headedness when it came to their new home. "We may have rushed our move into the cottage."

"We agreed that moving right in was the best option," Laura argued. Now that she was away from the mess, her earlier mood made perfect sense. Everyone felt overwhelmed when they were surrounded by boxes and a growing list of unexpected adjustments. Stepping away from it now would only delay having to deal with everything. Once she and Jay were unpacked and the cottage was tidy, Laura was sure that the rest would sort itself out. Sinking more money into different accommodations would only add to their stress. "With my workload dropping off so sharply and your job not due to begin for a few weeks, we need to watch the savings we have left."

"We do," Jay agreed even as he held up one hand to silence her. "But when we calculated our budget, it was based on the cottage being as problem-free as it looked. Now that we have had time to get a feel for the place, I don't believe it is. Whatever survey was done didn't show the issues we have already experienced. We know we need to have the wiring checked because the kitchen light is on the dodgy. I believe I caught a whiff of that smell you mentioned when I got up for a drink last night. Whatever is causing it can't be good. Flipping a light switch and burning the place down is a real concern. The draft turning random spots into the Arctic is most likely coming through some crack in the wall or up through the floorboards. Finding and fixing it is bound to be a major undertaking as well, and one that needs to be done before winter arrives. We both heard the plumbing knocking after my shower, so that is another thing that needs to be looked into. Especially since the sound seemed to come from a completely different location than it should be. I would have expected it behind the tiles, not from the opposite wall."

Jay didn't mention the nightmare or the dreadful feeling of being watched. Nor did he mention the face he still believed he saw at the window despite his lack of evidence. Laura didn't need to know those things yet. Jay wasn't prone to an overactive imagination. He didn't have an anxious temperament. That didn't mean that the new life they were embarking on couldn't have him unsettled enough to set his nerves on edge.

"I have only really noticed the light and the smell," Laura shook her head. Something about her thoughtful pause made Jay wonder if there was something she wasn't telling him. "The knocking was probably just me moving things around. But, I can agree that maybe the cottage needs a good going over and a bit of a renovation that will make settling in difficult. We just don't have many options. Especially if we can't put the improvements off until spring as we planned."

"We can stay at the inn," Jay reached down and stroked the terrier's ear. If Harvey could be his ally in this, he would use the excuse to its fullest. "Harvey is fine when he isn't surrounded by all of the chaos of our move. Did you know that I caught him growling at the door this morning when I made coffee? I thought he wanted out but when I offered to open it, he hid behind my legs and wouldn't budge."

"He isn't used to all the wildlife scents in the air," Laura scratched Harvey's head. He was such a good boy normally. "He probably smelled a fox. Once the local fauna learns there is a dog in residence, they will most likely keep to the woods. I feel for him. I do. But, unless Harvey is going to get a job and help pay the bills, staying at the inn and spending the money to handle renovations now will devour the rest of our savings."

"We will make it back," Jay assured her. "You get an earlier start on the video series while I still have a block of free time before the term starts. Two weeks of hard work now could get us farther ahead monetarily sooner than we planned for. Harvey can get used to his new home a little at a time and if he's having a bad day or we run into something he shouldn't be around, we can leave him at Penny's, the sitter. Plus, we get the bonus of a good night's sleep followed by breakfast that we don't have to prepare before we dive into the day's tasks. I wouldn't be pushing for this if I didn't firmly believe it's the right decision, Laura."

"And what about our things?" Laura asked. Jay was right, of course. He usually was about things like this. That didn't mean she had to like the idea.

Martin arrived with their plates and gave them a worried look.

"Eavesdropping is a hazard of the job," he said setting their plates down. "That being said, is everything okay at the cottage?"

"We were just discussing a change in our timeline for some renovations." Jay gave Laura a hopeful smile. "Well, I'm trying to sell the idea to my lovely wife, at any rate."

"Jay thinks we would be better off staying at the inn and handling some of the bigger projects now rather than holding off until spring or trying to live with the mess we are bound to make," Laura tried for a smile but the sadness she had woken to was back heavier than it had been before.

"I thought the place was in tip-top shape," Martin shrugged. "Then again, I haven't seen it since I was a boy and one of my friends dared me to knock on the door at midnight. That was a thing back then. Charlie swore that the door would swing open if I did and the whole place would light up."

"And did it?" Jay did his best to ignore the chill that ran up his spine. How he could wonder if such a wild story held any truth was beyond reason. That didn't keep the thought from taking root.

"Oh, I went to the cottage at midnight," Martin said conspiratorially. "I had to sneak out of my bedroom window to do it and wade through fog along the river walk. By the time I reached the cottage, whatever bravery I had was long gone. After about five minutes of staring at the door, I bolted when a twig snapped behind me and ran back home through the fields. I don't think I slept a wink that night. I kept waiting for the ghost of John Noble to loom over my bed and tell me he was going to take me out hunting. That was another old ghost story altogether but mixing the two made sense to my twelve-year-old brain. I ended up missing school the next day. By the time Charlie could ask me what happened, I had a grand old lie cobbled together to tell him. Then, I dared him to go. He never did. Then again, his bedroom window was higher up than mine was, so he had a ready-made excuse."

He laughed, but inside Laura and Jay had their

own private thoughts whirling around in their heads.

"Do you think the cottage is haunted Martin?" Laura was half laughing but her eyes betrayed fear.

"Oh, there are lots of stories about lots of the old houses around here. Same as any old building really, isn't it?" Matin's sentence seemed peter out.

"Most of the issues are probably just from disuse," Jay assured him. "A house with no one living inside it is always trying its best to go to seed. All it takes is a family of field mice to make their home in a place where they aren't noticed to set bigger problems in motion. The cottage has fine bones. We just need to tackle a few things that probably went unnoticed until we moved in."

"Makes sense," Martin shrugged. "If you need any help with it, ask around. Plenty of people in the village will lend a hand even if it is mostly just to satisfy their curiosity about you and the cottage."

"That reminds me," Laura interrupted with a question that had been on her mind most of the day. "How often do the locals use the Footpaths behind the cottage?"

"They don't," Martin shook his head. "Not openly, at least. I'm sure a few have snuck to the clearing to declare their love. That's a tradition around here, too. There is a bench out there that has led to more than one proposal over the years. Otherwise, people stick to the river walk and the Footpaths over the other side of the river. It's always been over grown behind your cottage, the path was never maintained there. Why do you ask?"

"Just curiosity," Laura said, although Jay picked up on something else. "We want to open them up so we can walk straight to the lake. They are public rights of way so I was just wondering if anyone would want to use them if we did. I've seen a younger man with two dogs along the river walk. I had the impression that he might be heading to, or coming from, the Footpath at the cottage. Do you know him?"

That was the same young man who hadn't waved at Jay. Why the memory of that small slight irked him so much was a mystery, but it did. Maybe it was that the man had waved at Laura the day before. Jay wasn't a jealous man. Laura gave him no reason to be. It was the face in the window, barely glimpsed the night before, and her coffee cup sitting in the sink. Combined with the rest of the oddities of the cottage, it wasn't a far stretch of the imagination to believe that some stranger had taken an unhealthy interest in Laura and found a way into their home. Just the thought renewed Jay's vigour for moving them both back to the inn for the time being.

"I can't say that I know anyone from the village that meets that description," Martin said thoughtfully. "It could be someone up from the surrounding villages I suppose. It's a bit of a trek just to walk your dogs, but Adington's river walk is pretty enough to warrant it. Still, without some sort of invitation to the property, you would think a man would be more respectful. There are plenty of signs marking that area as private land."

"You would think," Jay took a sip of his drink, wishing once again that he had ordered a pint and been done with it. His sour mood was only growing worse by the minute. "We may have to double-check that the signs are still in place. Not to sound unneighbourly, but I would like to get past the renovation and get settled before we need to think about socialising. Maybe we need to look at insurance or something?"

"That's a sound idea," Martin said as Laura frowned. "Even good intentions have their consequences. The last thing you need is someone breaking a leg out there and no one knowing about it for days."

"Exactly," Jay said, thankful for a far more logical argument than the one his imagination conjured.

"I know there are risks, Jay," Laura sighed once Martin went back to the bar. "I just hate that we need to look stand-offish about the Footpaths."

"Just for a bit," Jay took her hand and squeezed it softly. "We need time to get to know our new home, Laura. And we need to offer assurances to anyone who is on our land. We also need to know who they are. If the village pub owner in a village where news travels faster than light doesn't know someone, that makes me wonder about them even more. I'm not saying the man's trouble. I just think that getting to know him a bit before we let him into our space would be a good thing. Don't you?"

"Is there something you aren't telling me?" Laura cocked her head and squinted her eyes. Jay should have known she would sense that there was more behind his insistence.

"I don't think so," Jay waved her concern away. "Nothing but a night of poor sleep and a big job ahead that has me focusing on unforeseen problems. Before you know it, this little hiccup will be in the past and I will be back to my usual happy self."

"You don't think we made a mistake in buying the cottage, do you?" Laura asked softly. "I feel like I may have been so excited about it all that I missed some worry you had."

"You never miss a thing," Jay laughed. It was true. His beautiful wife knew him far too well to let anything slip by her. "And you didn't this time, either. Moving here is a big change, and our original timeline slipped a bit but that doesn't mean I regret anything. I'm just trying to make sure we get the best start in our new life as possible. The renovation may even provide more of an opportunity to get to know everyone faster since we will need both supplies and maybe a set of extra hands here and there. A plumber and an electrician, too. I know you are worried about the budget but hiring out some of the work will make it go faster. You want to be settled in just as much as I do."

"I do," Laura took a bite of her food and chewed thoughtfully. "So, now that I am forced to agree with you even though I hate the idea of having to live out of a suitcase again, maybe we should figure out our strategy. If you mean to have everything done before you start teaching, we don't have a lot of time to flail about. And we should both forget about restful nights and calm days. We know how renovations go. As soon as we touch the first thing, the whole

KEEPER'S COTTAGE

cottage will be in shambles as we try to fit in five more that we didn't plan for."

"There's my girl," relief washed through Jay like a tidal wave. Even if the renovation proved to require gutting the cottage, that would be fine. Paranoia or not, staying at the inn would provide a bubble of safety for Laura just in case there was more of a threat than old wiring or faulty plumbing going on within its walls. The people of Adington were admittedly curious and unashamed of it. Jay was sure that by evening, Martin would have brought the man with the dogs to everyone's attention. Then, it was only a matter of time before Jay's concerns were either laid to rest or proven to be more than a lingering fantasy brought on by a nightmare.

"You've got that look again," Laura poked his hand bringing his attention back from its dark wanderings.

"What look is that Love?" Jay knew full well that his mind had drifted to suspicious places. For a moment, he considered telling her about the dream and the face and how mention of the stranger felt like a puzzle piece falling into place. She would understand. The problem was, he didn't. Not yet.

125

Throwing that kind of accusation out into the light of day with so little to back it up was ridiculous.

"The one that says you are getting ready to go into battle," Laura raised an eyebrow.

"Well, we are, aren't we?" He grinned, eyes sparkling. "Two weeks to win against an icy draft, thumping pipes, and whatever rodents have gained the high ground in our electrical system. I may not be some famous general off to change the world but as a lover of history, I can't help but see the challenges ahead and get a bit of a thrill. Besides, my warrior princess will be at my side through it all. How can a man not get a bit lost in the idea of that?"

"Only you could turn a handful of house projects into some sort of revolution," Laura laughed so hard she had to put down her fork. The sound of it cleared the last of the foul mood lingering in the air between them. "Alright, General Jay. Where do we start?"

Two days later, and with a solid schedule in mind, Jay and Laura set to work. Harvey was off on a playdate at the sitters. He hadn't even wanted to go in the cottage long enough for Jay and Laura to pack their clothes. Instead, he sat outside whining and barking at the air until they were well up the drive. As soon as they reached the road, he settled down and pranced the rest of the way with his ball held firmly in his jaws. Neither of them commented on the oddness of his behaviour. There didn't seem to be much point to it. Whatever had the terrier so put off about the cottage would surely be gone once the renovation was finished. If not, they would handle his issues then.

"We officially have a storage room instead of a bedroom," Laura handed Jay the last of the boxes and leaned against the doorframe. "The plumber is scheduled for the end of the week, and the electrician for next Monday."

"The new tiles should arrive by Friday," Jay gave one last look at the stack of boxes filling their room behind him and eased the door shut. "I want to pull up a few floorboards in both the bathroom and the office before we get too far into the rest. We need to know if there is an issue with the crawl space or even the possibility of a cellar that was closed off and not recorded. Plus, it will give me a good look at the foundation. Did you find someone to check the chimney?"

"Tuesday," Laura rolled her shoulders hoping to release some of the building tension resting between them. Two weeks wasn't enough time. Not when Jay was going to pull up the floor. The plumber wanted the plaster removed from the wall where the knocking sound came from along with all of the tiles in the rest of the room. The electrician required access to the wires running to all of the outlets and switches. She hadn't been able to find a contractor who could fit in the repairs before the end of the month. Nor was she able to locate a builder who could look for telltale signs of crumbling mortar on the exterior of the cottage. On top of all of that, it felt like her desire to leave her new home as original as possible was out of reach. Although she wasn't often prone to crying, she felt tears stinging her eyes.

"Hey now," Jay wrapped his arms around her and held her close. "We've got this."

"Not in two weeks, we don't, Jay." Laura sniffled and burrowed her face into his big, solid chest. "Not when we have so much to do. And when we are finished, the cottage is going to be unrecognisable. It just breaks my heart. I thought the changes would happen over time. Now, here we are, stripping out the past as quickly as possible."

"A few tiles don't change the bones of the place," Jay stroked her back. "And you have to admit that you hate the olive green. You make a face at it every time you walk into the bath or the backsplash in the kitchen catches your attention. This is a good thing,

Laura. It's a fresh start. Better to get the work behind us so we can enjoy our new home more fully."

"I know," Laura leaned back and gave him a sad smile. "It's just a lot."

"Why don't you go find us some lunch? I'll get started so you won't have to be the one to make the first change. That should take a bit of pressure off, don't you think?" A bubble of winter air drifted over them causing Laura to shiver in his arms. There was a faint thump from somewhere in the walls as it disappeared. Jay had to force his jaw to relax when he caught his teeth grinding.

"No," Laura stepped back. "I'm not hungry right now. If you are, I'll get you something. I just want to get started on my part. Broken heart or not, every-thing on the list needs to be done. I know that."

"I'm good as well," Jay's stomach was back to its angry churning. He would have eaten if Laura was hungry but on his own, he would rather wait until some progress was made. "Why don't you start on the ugly tiles in the bath? We will see how far we can get before hunger sets in. Then, we can take a break with dinner at the pub and give Harvey a nice walk before diving back in."

The time flew by once they got started. Although

Laura couldn't find a reason for the icy draft no matter how many tiles she removed from the walls, she had to admit that the ease with which the olive green squares fell away was alarming. She barely had to touch one with the chisel before it landed in her hand. Not a single one cracked. Nor was the grout difficult to scrape away. She stacked them in a neat pile thinking she would find some new use for them in the garden when spring came. It seemed like a good compromise. She could pay homage to the original structure in a fountain or some other feature where the colour would blend with its surroundings instead of having the dark olive tone steal light from the rooms inside.

Jay, on the other hand, had the full weight of the battle he had been so excited to enter on his hands. Everything he touched was ten times more difficult than it should have been. The plaster walls were as hard as bedrock. The nails in the floorboards held tight forcing him to use all his strength along with the long crowbar. By the time they locked the cottage door, he was more than ready for a break.

"There's the man with the dogs again," Laura said waving as they walked back from a hearty meal and a mellowing pint to wash it down. The man waved back but immediately turned away when Jay raised his hand. "Maybe we should catch up to him. Something about him seems so familiar to me although I can't tell you why."

"Hm," Jay grunted. He made himself shake off the unsettling urge to chase after the man and demand to know if he had been the one at the window. Laura's comment did nothing to ease his mind. "I think we should. If nothing else, we may have a name to put to his face."

No matter how fast they walked, they couldn't close the distance between the man and his two large dogs. Then, they lost him completely as a group of villagers passed in the opposite direction blocking their view. Jay was sure the trio hadn't been close enough to the Footpaths to disappear into the trees. Still, no amount of searching brought him into sight.

"He must have doubled back along the river bank," Laura turned to scan the area behind them but saw no hint of the stranger there either. "Or he crossed the river walk and went through the fields into the village. If he's from Keterton, he most likely brings a car. Maybe that's the quickest way back to it.

"Tomorrow," Jay assured her. He was even more determined to talk to the man face to face now than he had been before. "Or the next day, if it comes to that. I think we should make it a point to meet him."

"We have a storm and torrential rain coming later," Laura turned back with a shrug. Nobody could just disappear. There must be some path that she and Jay hadn't noticed before. "The local weather says we are under a flood watch for the next few days."

"It's a good thing that we know the cottage roof doesn't leak at least, and its far enough up the hill not to flood." Letting his concern about the stranger and his dogs slide back to the corner of his mind, Jay took Laura's hand and nudged her shoulder playfully.

"Bite your tongue before you tempt fate," Laura nudged him back.

That night the storm kept them both awake, the rain hammering on the window as if it was trying to break in. By morning the wind had died a little but still the rain persisted. The river lapped at its banks and the flow was faster than they had ever seen it. Jay and Laura needed to get on, they were on a tight schedule and weather couldn't lose them a day. They left early for a supply run in local village shop ahead of what was becoming their habit to stop in the pub each day. Jay wanted to take the car but found the battery dead when he got in to start it. They would have to just get on and walk to the cottage. Rain coats and brollies, they set off.

The banks had broken and the fields were starting to flood. "By the time we come home later, that water is going to have completely flooded our way home, we will have to come back the road way" Jay said

"Wait," Laura grabbed his arm. As she turned, she caught movement out of the corner of her eye. Someone was out in the floodwater. "Jay, there is someone out there. It's...I think it's that man. I can see two dark heads just above the water beside him. They are going to be swept away!"

"Oh bloody hell, what is he doing he's going to drown out there. Quick Laura go get help from the pub, I'll call 999 and try to get his attention."

"Jay, you can't go in there!" Laura tugged at Jay's arm trying to pull him away. "We'll go back to the village together. We'll get help."

Jay inched his way closer to the water's rushing edge. The man was up to his waist already. The dogs beside him barely had their heads above it. He called out but doubted he could be heard over the rain pounding down on the fast current.

"Go, Laura!" Jay turned to his wife. "I'm not fool

enough to get too close. Someone needs to keep an eye on them, though."

She cursed loudly and then took off like a shot, running through the pounding rain. When Jay turned back, the man and his dogs were gone. Jay raced back along the river walk scanning the current that had swept them away for any sign of life. He saw nothing.

Search crews were called out but no sign of the man or his dogs were found. Days passed and no missing person report was filed. Although the story was the talk of the village, no one knew the identity of the missing man. Nor could they explain why he and his dogs had simply disappeared. The river walk took on an eerie quality as the story spread and the speculations grew in strangeness. The whole episode only amplified the disquiet Jay and Laura felt at the cottage. It was yet another strange occurrence that had no answer hovering over the growing mess of a renovation.

CHAPTER

SEVEN

1954

Peter's first thought when his employer eased him away from the crowds and far from prying eyes and ears was for Jane. Something had gone very wrong. He wasn't sure exactly what at first, but he knew from the hard glint in John Noble's eyes that the trouble led straight back to him. Jane was the only point of contention there could be. Every other aspect of Peter's life and work on the estate was running smoothly.

"You will show me the note that my daughter passed to you," John said once they were away from the festivities. "Do not make things worse by trying to hide it. I will know what is going on before it ruins the girl's future."

"There is no note, sir," Peter assured him quickly. It wasn't a lie. The words in question were already ash in the bottom of the bonfire burning at the centre of the festival. Peter had made sure of it by using Jane's heartfelt plea as a means to light the fire. He would not go so far as to lie and say it had never existed but with no proof to prove it had, Peter didn't feel compelled to do more.

"She's a silly girl, Peter. Silly girls make mistakes and can be forgiven their impetuousness," John Noble was holding his temper by the barest of threads. It was obvious in the way the vein in his temple pulsed. "Any man who encourages them does so at his peril. Countries have fallen because some man was foolish enough to indulge the fancies of a woman. And do we blame the woman for this? No. Because men should know better, they always carry the consequences."

"You have no reason to believe Jane has done anything wrong." Peter shook his head. "Where is this coming from?"

"Jane turned down a proposal from a suiter who has done nothing but show her that she could be happy with him," John's words stabbed directly into Peter's heart. "Richard Fields was all but made for Jane. He could have curbed her wilder side without causing her to feel stifled. She should have been dancing for joy. Instead, she ran from the room as if she had been set ablaze as soon as the question was posed. There is no explanation for that outside the one I was given."

"Which is?" Peter asked. In his heart, he already knew the answer. Jane would never have married another while she was so deeply in love with him. She would have refused to lie that lie or to force any man who sought a marriage with her to play second fiddle to the one that held her heart. She did not have the ability for that kind of deceit in her makeup.

"That there is something devious between the two of you. Some secret. A father knows in his heart that the only kind of secret that could be is one where you have encouraged his daughter's idiotic affections," he poked an angry finger against Peter's chest. "You are pale as a ghost, Peter Marsh. That tells me that there is truth to the accusation."

"And just who told you these things?" It had to be Sally. There was no one else. He and Jane had been far too careful in their interactions. Sally was the only one who could have seen the note being passed and she was spiteful enough to use that knowledge in the worst possible way.

"It doesn't matter," John said through gritted teeth.

"It does if the source has a vested interest in causing trouble," Peter insisted. He had to convince Jane's father that there was another explanation for her sake. Peter had never seen the man so angry. A month ago, he would have sworn John Noble had no temper at all. "I was just about to break off a relationship that was going nowhere. The girl knows it's coming and has a vengeful disposition. If this so-called information came from her, you should take it with a very large grain of salt."

What would that anger do if it was turned on Jane? Since the festival began and Richard Fields came on the scene, Peter had seen her anxiety. It rested just below the surface of her new clothes and perfectly applied powder. She was struggling to be someone she wasn't just to keep up appearances. The hand she had used to beg him to run away with her was shaking and hurried as she scrawled the words across the page. Peter had seen enough to know that Richard was not the direct cause. Jane was in a beautiful prison designed by her father. It was crushing her spirit. Barring a mad dash in the middle of the night, the only escape open to her was to walk to the alter beside a man she barely knew.

Peter would burn down the world before he saw that happen. His love for Jane gave him no other choice.

Peter kept his face carefully calm. John Noble was a father precariously balanced on the edge of reason because his daughter would not see the fine logic and care he had used in planning her future. Never mind that it was a future that he had given Jane no say in. John expected her to rejoice in his efforts and embrace the outcome with a full and willing heart. That much was as certain as the fact that he had convinced himself that she would. Now that she hadn't, someone else had to be to blame. There was no other option. He wasn't looking for the truth as far as Jane and Peter's affair went. That would pose too many uncomfortable questions. It would force John to see that he was not nearly as interested in Jane's happiness as he was in his own. The temper Peter saw now was nothing more than a way for John to avoid that ugly truth. Peter was already the target. His employer now only had one option. He had to prove he was right by removing the one obstacle he had convinced himself stood in the way of his perfect plan coming to fruition. He would not be looking for proof of an affair, only an excuse to remove a potential rival from the field.

Once that was accomplished, all would be well once more, or so he believed. When that didn't happen, John Noble would explode and his beloved daughter would be caught in the centre of his destruction. Peter had to find a way to keep that from happening. He at least had to find a way to remove Jane before it did. Her sister, too, if possible. With him and Jane out of the picture, Sarah would take the brunt of it.

Ordinarily, the festival would have provided ample opportunity to slip away. There were crowds to blend with. There was traffic to hide their departure. There was reason to leave on errands that they would never return from. This year was different. Jane was on a tight leash, and her father held it in a vice-like grip.

For a brief moment, Peter considered whether Richard might be an ally. He believed the man was just as much a pawn in the high-stakes game John played. Nothing about the man's behaviour toward Jane made Peter believe that Richard had any hand in the scheme. If anything, Richard had been lied to, just to prompt the fast proposal. He was from a good family with money at his disposal and a brain in his head. Peter had seen more than one longing look in his direction from the women who saw him. There would have been no reason for him to rush into such an important decision unless he firmly believed that the marriage was agreeable to both sides and stood to benefit them equally. Ultimately, Peter couldn't justify pulling the man further into the chaos by enlisting his aid. With any luck at all, Richard would already be on his way home and away from the problem entirely.

"I am willing to give this situation until the end of the week. As I said, Jane is a silly girl just like most girls her age. She can be allowed that long to come to her senses without causing more of a stir. You, on the other hand...If I find any hint of proof that you have done anything to corrupt my daughter or threaten her standing in society, rest assured that your job here is over. Your reputation will be shattered. I will ensure that you never find work as a gamekeeper again. No respectable family will employ you because I will warn them about your penchant for vulnerable young ladies and your willingness to lead them astray. Jane can survive the scandal of falling victim to your nefarious ways. I can ensure that any part she played was small and only engaged in under your coercion. Such a thing may even settle her impetuous side once the dust settles. The same does not go for the hired help that overstepped his place and tried to bring ruin on the family who gave him steady work and a roof over his head." John stood up straight and gave the jacket he wore a tug. He held Peter's gaze as he straightened his tie. "One whiff of verification that this rumour may hold fact, and by the time I am finished with you, you'll be lucky to land a job hosing down the floors at the slaughterhouse. Have I made myself clear?"

"Perfectly, sir," Peter said. He was secretly amazed that his employer had been able to think through the problem and its solution so clearly considering the state he was in. What John proposed could very well work out exactly as he said. All anyone needed was a juicy story with a clearly defined victim and a dastardly villain to let any scandal run its course quickly and cleanly. Jane could be the darling of the peerage by the end of it all if her father played his cards right and Peter took a hard enough fall.

As the man Peter no longer felt he knew turned away and put his mask of civility back in place, Peter knew beyond the shadow of a doubt that his time in Adington was over. He also knew that he had the hardest decision in his life to make. He wasn't a fool and he wasn't blind. The last week had shown him just how far Jane's father was willing to go to see his eldest daughter married off to the right kind of man. One week. What father expected his flesh and blood to tie themselves to someone they had only just met? Jane had been dressed in fancy clothes that might accentuate her form but didn't fit her nature. She had been paraded around and forced to behave in ways that ill-suited her free spirit. The man at her arm seemed decent enough, but it was obvious to anyone who truly looked that Jane saw him in the same light as a cousin at best. There was no budding love there. There was no hint of desire. Peter would have seen it. He would have felt the ache in his heart if such affection existed.

Certainty of the course Peter had to take settled into place. Jane loved him. She belonged with him. Peter had tried to fight it even when he had her in his arms. He had tried to convince himself that he could let her go when the time came. The lie no longer held water. John Noble had punched far too many holes in it. Peter and Jane were meant to be together just as she had claimed all along. He could not leave her here to face a future designed by someone who refused to see her for who she was any more than he could enlist a fox's help to guard the pheasants.

The end of the festival was only two days away.

Surely that would give him enough time to sort out a plan. They could elope and start their life as man and wife far away from the fury he had just witnessed. Jane said she would come to him when the fair was over. He could be ready by then. He could find a way to get word to her. If they needed to wait a bit longer, he would just keep pretending that the rumour was nothing more than a spiteful girl stirring up trouble until a moment came when he and Jane could sneak away. She had to do her part to ease her father's fears until then. All he had to do was find a way to let her know.

Peter went back to his duties feeling as if everyone he passed was watching his every move. It was a ridiculous notion. Neither the Nobles nor the Fields would have broadcast the problem of Jane's refusal. Even Sally would not be stupid enough to risk the wrath of her betters by openly passing the rumour along. Not this quickly. There was too much value in the secret, still. None of that did anything to stop the itch between his shoulder blades as if some dagger hovered just above his flesh.

Two days. He could pull himself together and ride it out. Then, he and Jane would be off to a new life. That was what mattered. Not this small bit of discomfort.

It took most of the day but Peter finally shook the irritating feeling of being watched. His dreams were still troubled that night but he chalked it up to worry over Jane. By breakfast, he had himself convinced that the worst of it had blown over. He started his day early with the dogs at his side and had everything well in hand by the time the first vendors began showing up.

"You look mighty calm for someone about to lose his job, Peter Marsh," Sally said smugly as she passed him with a basket of fresh bread. "And here I was thinking you were just sulking because I made you eat breakfast at your own table when you were really chasing after the boss's daughter. For shame."

"So, it was you who convinced Mr. Noble that your nasty little rumour was worth listening to," Peter shook his head. "I told him as much, you know."

"What I know is what I saw," Sally gave him an evil little grin. "Not just yesterday, either. The two of you weren't nearly as careful as you thought with your little fling. That little note pass just allowed me to see the larger picture of your naughty little interactions. I've seen you walking too close together by the river. Then, there was the time Mother had me deliver bread. It was far too early for anyone to be awake at the big house, yet Jane was walking to the back door in the same clothes she had on the day before. I'm not blind, Peter. I'm not stupid, either. She was on the path that led to your cottage. I know what the two of you were up to. I was willing to hold my tongue - for a while at least. I still haven't told Mr. Noble about her early morning return through the back door so she wouldn't be seen. He was mad enough over the rest. I thought that might put him right over the edge."

"Perhaps she couldn't sleep and was out for an early morning stroll before breakfast? There are plenty of places that path leads other than to my door." Peter wished he had never crossed paths with the little viper. How he had ever thought Sally was beautiful was something he couldn't explain now. She was rotten to the core and it was written all over her face. "Whatever it is that you want, Sally, I don't have it. Mr. Noble isn't going to deliver it into your hands, either. The only thing you'll get for spreading rumours like that is a worse reputation than the one you already have. People will tolerate a spoiled girl so long as she is pretty. Cruelty is another thing alto-gether. If you go after Jane like this, that is what you'll be known for. Every minute of the rest of your life, you will be the horrid little gossip who will say whatever she believes will get her what she wants."

"Better than being the disgraced gamekeeper who was toying with a fine lady's affections," Sally shrugged. She didn't even have the decency to blush as Peter called her out for her wickedness. "If I were you, I would leave now. I would go far, far away. Canada, maybe, or America. You might be able to get out from under the shadow of this scandal once you cross the ocean."

"There is no scandal aside from the one you are trying to start. Go sell your bread. So long as you leave Jane alone, I don't care what you do. If you need to go after me, so be it." Peter was disgusted. "I don't know if you thought this was a way to get me to pay more attention to you, but if you did, you were wrong. I'm finished being led around by the likes of you. I just want to do my job and live my life in peace. Go find some other use for your time, Sally. Maybe grow a soul while you are at it. Whatever you have now is an ugly little shrivelled thing that isn't doing you any good at all."

"You'll be sorry, Peter Marsh," Sally called after him. "You just wait. You'll wish with all of your heart that you never threw me aside. I am the best thing that could ever happen to you. We could have clawed our way out of this stupid village and made something of ourselves. You'll never do that without me pushing you. You'll see."

Peter made his way toward the pheasant pens. There were birds to see to before the festival goers arrived. The beginning of what promised to be an epic headache was pounding at his temples. To make matters worse, the estate's stable hand was leaning against the shed door. That could only mean that there was more stress about to land in his lap.

"Sean, what can I do for you?" Peter asked. They got on well enough but hadn't done more than share the neighbouring barstools at the pub since Peter hired on. Sean rarely had reason to visit the pens just as Peter seldom went to the stables.

"Mr. Noble sent word that he wants to take some guests on a small shoot at the clearing this morning. Nothing big. Ten or fifteen birds will do with a small set-up in the usual spot. He's got three sportsmen coming in from out of town that should be here within the hour. It's meant to be a sample shoot to encourage them to schedule a larger outing in a few weeks." Sean looked as if his head might be thumping at the same tempo that Peter's was.

"He sent word through you?" Normally, even

such a spontaneous event would have brought John Noble to Peter's door or vice versa.

"I offered," Sean nodded his head toward the stables. "He came to see about horses just as the blacksmith was setting up for a reshoeing. We worked hoof maintenance into the festival as an exhibition this year. I needed a break from the noise and the general mood of the estate. The whole place feels like a storm's about to break. Not that I'm one for carrying tales, but something went wrong inside the big house and whatever it is has everyone's teeth on edge."

"I could use help making this shoot look like I had a week to plan it instead of an hour if you can spare the time," Peter offered. He knew exactly what had gone wrong in the Noble home but wasn't about to share any details. With some luck, everything would all simmer down before they got worse. By then, he and Jane would be long gone.

"I'll take you up on that with thanks," Sean nodded. "Tell me what you need from me."

Peter sent Sean out to ready the clearing while he gathered the birds. With such short notice, it would be a miracle if everything happened as it was supposed to. Even so small of a group shoot required a day or two of planning. The festival going on at the same time complicated it all the more. The clearing was far enough from the main event to be at a safe distance provided no one snuck off into the woods for one reason or another. The only thing going for him in that category was that it was early enough in the day and late enough in the festival itself that most of those planning to attend wouldn't arrive until afternoon. Any couples sneaking into the trees for a moment of privacy were far more likely to wait until evening came. That, along with some strict safety rules that he planned to lay down when he met the group with the horses they would use to reach the clearing, was the best he could do on such short notice.

Sarah was petting her dappled mare when Peter entered the stable. She opened her mouth when he came in but then closed it quickly and shook her head. She looked worried. Peter had very little doubt of the cause.

Peter nodded a greeting to her and kept his mouth shut as well. At this point, he wasn't about to stick his foot further in the muck than it already was, nor was he going to drag the poor girl into the mess swirling around her.

"The horses you are looking for are in the yard out back," she said finally. Her normally soft voice sounded strained today as if the words she said were trying desperately to keep others from leaving her lips. "Sean had them saddled and ready before he went to find you. I thought it would be him that came and got them. Peter..."

Her voice trailed off and the worry he was doing his best to pretend wasn't plain to see deepened. He wasn't sure if he should ask if there was a problem or if he should just keep his mouth shut and let things play out as they would.

"Father wants you to fail today," Sarah said before he could think of the right question to ask her. She peered into the dark corners of the barn as if searching for someone who might overhear. "He doesn't always think that I hear things, but I do. I've heard a lot since yesterday that I find troubling. It isn't my place to voice my opinion on any of it but I do think that you deserve a bit of warning when it comes to this shoot. I believe that the reason it was set up so quickly is so Father has a reason to fire you. I can't be sure of that, of course."

"I understand," Peter thought as much while he was gathering the birds. Failure to secure a larger event because of an unimpressive morning would be the perfect grounds to sack him. "And I thank you for the warning. I've got things as well in hand as I am able. Beyond that, today will be what today will be."

"One more thing," Sarah said in a tense whisper as he passed her.

"Yes?" Peter busied himself checking the mare's tack as if that was his entire reason for stopping to speak to the girl.

"If - and I am not saying this is true by any means - just if," Sarah faltered before taking a deep breath and rushing through the rest of what she had to say. "If there is real love between two people and those two people felt that they needed to hide it from everyone else, it would make me very sad for them. I would understand if they were to want to start a life together somewhere else, although that would make me sad as well. I would never think badly of them. If one of them needed to get a message to the other to answer a question that may have been posed about this matter, they could simply leave my mare's harness on the bench if that answer was yes or hang it back on the hook if it was no."

She gave him a very piercing look that was well beyond her years before rushing out of the stables. Peter felt a tight knot form in his throat. He did not doubt Sarah's intentions. She was without guile and loved her sister greatly. Peter let his fingers slide over the smooth leather while he pulled himself together. This was what he needed most. Sarah had offered him a way to answer Jane.

Reverently, Peter laid the harness on the bench, letting his hand linger for longer than necessary while his heartbeat slowed back to a normal pace. Then, he went to get the horses.

"Good morning, gentlemen," Peter said with a much warmer smile than he had been able to conjure only moments ago. "My name is Peter Marsh. I am the gamekeeper for the Noble estate, and I will be leading your pheasant shoot today. But first, I would like to go over a few extra precautions that must be taken before we go to the clearing where your birds await."

There was a general murmur of greeting and some good-natured banter as the group gathered around him. Peter noticed that instead of three shooters, there were four but that wouldn't matter. There would be enough birds to go around and enough refreshments to content the party. He had anticipated some small changes to the count with such short notice. There always seemed to be someone who decided to join in at the last minute and he rarely got any notice of the change until he did a head count.

John Noble was the last to arrive. Peter wondered at the absence of any representation from the Field's estate but let the matter go almost as soon as the question came to mind. After Jane's refusal, there was a high likelihood that the family had gone home to avoid any further awkwardness.

"Good morning, Mr. Noble," Peter kept his tone professional. He might be expected to fail but that didn't mean he had to add any hint of discord to the morning. "I was just about to go over some added safety concerns since we will be holding the morning's shoot at the same time as the festival."

John nodded and motioned for him to go on as he adjusted the rifle he carried. Peter did his best to ignore the new tension that permeated the air with his employer's arrival. Hopefully, he was the only one who felt it. The last thing anyone needed was antsy men with guns less than a mile away from the fair.

"If everyone would turn toward the far lawn, I would like you to ensure that all ammunition and casings have been removed from your rifles and that the barrel is clear of obstruction. Once that is verified, please stow your arms in their cases. We will be riding through the main body of the festival and want to remove any chance of an accident there. Once we get to the clearing, we will focus our shots toward the west side of the estate, away from the Footpaths as an added precaution."

Peter noticed John was having a hard time getting the breach to open on his rifle. Thinking there might be a jam, he walked over to offer his assistance as he would with anyone else. Just as he stepped around to the far side, John turned and raised the muzzle as if trying to get a better angle.

The world exploded with a deafening crack as the rifle went off. The pressure that stole Peter's breath away knocked him backward. As he fell, searing pain radiated out from the centre of his chest. He didn't understand at first. The shock was far too great to make sense of what was happening. His vision went dark around the edges and the taste of copper filled his mouth.

"Jane," he whispered as her father knelt beside him.

"Yes, Jane," John Noble growled with a look of horrified satisfaction in his eyes. "You left me no choice, boy. None at all. For that, may we both be damned."

There were running footsteps and an anguished

scream. Peter tried to reach out but his hand was too heavy to lift. Then, the scent of the woman he loved enveloped him and the warmth of her body gathered him close.

"What have you done? Father, what have you done?!" Jane was sobbing. Her tears fell like molten gold onto Peter's skin. "Peter! Oh, Peter, don't leave me. Please, please, don't leave me. I love you. Please. Stay with me. Just stay with me."

Peter heard everything around him as if in a dream. His vision cleared although curiously, what he saw made no sense. Jane cradled his body, rocking as if soothing a child to sleep. John Noble did his best to pull her away. Others came at a run. Richard, first. Then Sarah, who he blocked before she could get close enough to see the cause of all the commotion.

"Get my father," Richard told Sarah pushing her back the way she came. "Call an ambulance."

Peter saw it all from above as if he were a bird. He felt strangely calm. The broken, bloody body in Jane's arms meant nothing to him. Only the woman who held it had meaning now. He reached down and brushed invisible fingers over her soft cheek. Her breath hitched and her eyes closed before she lifted her face to the sky and keened.

"It was an accident," John Noble announced. "I didn't know the boy was there. He should have never been there in the first place. I was trying to verify the rifle was empty. That's all. I didn't know it was loaded. I never leave my guns loaded. They are always cleaned after a shoot and stored safely. I have no idea how this could have happened."

"I saw, Father," Jane said softly. Then louder, nearly a scream. "I saw. I know. No matter what anyone else believes, I know it was no accident. I know what you did. I hope you rot in hell for it."

"Come away now, Jane," Richard Fields stepped between the girl and her father as John's mouth worked silently trying to form a response to the accusation. "We will sort this out. There is nothing you can do for Peter now. Come away. Sarah is just inside. She will see to you. You shouldn't be here right now. I will get you inside with your sister. Then, I will come back and see to things out here. The ambulance is on its way."

"He killed Peter, Richard," Jane sobbed as she let Richard untangle her from Peter's body. She was covered in blood, her eyes were wild and her face as pale as a sheet. "All because I loved a gamekeeper where I couldn't love you or anyone else. Father killed him because I loved him. Oh, God, what have I done? It's all my fault. I'm sorry, Peter. I'm so sorry. I never thought this would happen. Never. I swear it. I thought we would run away together. I thought we would be happy. I never..."

Richard turned to John as Peter watched from above as Jane's words trailed off into anguished tears. When John Noble looked away first, Peter heard Richard curse beneath his breath. He turned back to Jane and gently eased her away from the body lying across her blood-soaked lap. Richard lifted her and she immediately fell limp, her eyelids fluttering and her face so pale that it appeared translucent.

"I won't leave you, Love," Peter promised. "I'll live in your heart. Let it be enough."

Peter was suddenly very tired. The world around him grew brighter until the scene below was washed away. Somehow, he knew that his Jane would be taken care of. It was a promise that entered his heart with such intensity that there was no arguing it. Peter let himself drift away with that thought, even as he clung to the promise he had made to her. He would not leave her, not really.

Not now.

Not ever.

CHAPTER

EIGHT

Present day

Autumn set in overnight. With it, the cottage took on ominous new habits. Laura didn't say this out loud. Neither did Jay although he thought the same. They walked hand in hand to the Hare, a few drinks and a relax was in order. There was a new face stood at the bar and Martin immediately introduced him. "Jay, Laura, this is Charlie, we go back years, since school, he used to work on the estate here. Laura and Jay live in Keepers Cottage, Charlie"

"Remember me telling you about him? This old bugger was the kid who dared me to knock on your cottage door when we were kids."

"Oh yes, I remember you telling us," Laura

laughed, "you got away lightly there Charlie." Jay ordered their drinks. "Do you still live locally Charlie?"

"Not far, but I've not been here the last few months as I have been staying with my son in Australia, just got back at the weekend. So how are you getting on at the cottage, seen the ghost yet?" Charlie laughed and took a drink. Laura wasn't laughing.

"I think I may have, well, felt it around anyway?"

Martin piped up then. "Oh, ignore Charlie, he's got so many stories about this village, half of them are made up and the other half aren't true".

Laura insisted. "No Really, I am interested Charlie, what is the history of our house?"

"Well, John Noble owned the estate in the 50s, he could never rest easy as he was thought to have killed Peter Marsh, the game keeper who lived in your cottage." Laura and Jay were looking in horror at this revelation.

"Not in our house?" Laura almost screamed the question. "No no, he shot him, he claimed "by mistake" out on a shoot, but folks don't think it was by mistake at all."

"His daughters still live nearby," Martin said.

"They are two of the loveliest ladies you could ever hope to meet. They run that coffee and cake meet up to raise funds for the village, you are bound to bump into them. They come here for Sunday lunch once a month too. The younger sister, Sarah, married Richard, the son of the neighbouring estate. Her children are about to hand running it down to the grandkids from what I hear. The older sister, Jane, well she never married, and moved in with Sarah and Richard." "Although I'm sure there are multiple versions of the story," Charlie continued, "the one I learned was that Jane was madly in love with Peter Marsh, and he with her. Peter was the gamekeeper for the estate and lived in the cottage you bought. John Noble tried to arrange for Jane to marry Richard, but she refused his proposal and embarrassed the family. When John found out the reason why was her relationship with Peter, well he shot him."

"Shot him?" Laura asked.

''Yes, one day during the autumn festival, he arranged a shoot, and at some point, during that shoot his gun went off and shot Peter and killed him. He claimed it was an accident and the verdict he received backed that up. Jane said differently and never spoke to her father again. By the end of it, there was enough of a question over what happened floating around the village that John Noble left for London and never came back. Eventually, the estate went to the sisters who sold most of it off, although Jane held on to the cottage and the woods behind it. So, I would say the rumour of her love affair with the gamekeeper is true. That's why it surprises me that there are problems with the place" Martin continued whilst he fed Harvey treats, "She had someone over there every year to see that it was kept in good order. I would have bet the Saturday night takings that your cottage was in better shape than any other buildings in the village."

Jay and Laura were quiet for a moment. "So, what do the stories say about the ghost, or ghosts?" Jay asked tentatively. "Is it John Noble or Peter or both? Who's seen them?"

"Well, there is a ghost walk in the village on Halloween, and Budgie Kirton the vicar tells ghost stories, and Lynn his wife runs a plant and cake stalls to raise funds for the church. "Budgie" Laura quizzed. "No idea why he's called Budgie no one does, it's all tongue in cheek you know. But he says poor Peter Marsh and his 2 black labs have been

KEEPER'S COTTAGE

seen walking by the river by several folk who have lived in the village over the years. He was only a young lad when he was shot, he's buried in the village church here"

THEY DRANK their pints in silence, neither wanted to admit, to say the words or even imagine they had seen the ghost of Peter Marsh. They walked back to the Inn and Jay said he thought they were making it up to scare them. There was obviously a guy they knew who walked his dogs by the river.

"But what about the man and his dogs we saw that day in the river, the disappeared and no trace ever found, no one reported missing. We even questioned if we had actually seen them at all or if it was a trick of the light. It's all very odd and deeply unsettling Jay, we need to find out more. What if Peter is haunting our cottage?"

"Laura stop, this is crazy, there are no such things as ghosts. Come on, you are believing some old folk who are having a joke at our expense. Maybe it's some kind of weird initiation to the village. The guy with the dogs' waves to you Laura and you wave back, and he ignores me, ghosts don't do that.

Laura was enraged by this comment. "You are

seriously jealous of a man who walks his dog and waves at me Jay, have you lost your bloody mind?"

"No, not jealous in the slightest, but worried he is some kind of stalker. Laura, look I think I saw him looking in the window of our house. Remember that night you found me outside naked? Well, I saw a face at the window in the kitchen, I ran outside to catch him, but he had gone"

"Oh Jay, you were going to run after a guy naked, what the hell were you going to do, scare him away?" They both started laughing and the near argument was diffused. Laura then admitted the incident in the kitchen when she thought she saw someone outside too.

"Ok, so here's what we need to do, I am going to go and talk to Martin at the pub tomorrow and tell him what's been happening, hopefully he will fess up and tell us who this man is. I will ask him to talk to him and tell him to stop the joke now, it's gone too far. Jay had gone into his "Get this shit sorted mode". Laura loved it when he took control of a situation and made it right.

Laura agreed, but she had her own plans, and tomorrow she was going to walk to the church and find Peters grave.

. . .

KEEPER'S COTTAGE

IT HAD BEEN A GOOD MORNING; they had both worked hard in the cottage and things were coming together a little more. Laura left Jay pulling up floorboards to get Harvey out for a walk before the rain was due later that afternoon.

Pulling up the floor in the office only revealed a bone-dry crawl space with one small, abandoned mouse nest beneath the window. There were no cracks in the foundation where a draft could sneak in, the earth beneath the cottage was reasonably warm. Still, there were pockets of icy air floating through their new home. Finding the reason was driving Jay mad. As he was sat with a tea in hand staring at the floor he had just pulled up, puzzling over his next move, he heard the front door open. "That was quick," he shouted, "Is it raining already?" No answer. "Laura, you ok?" He got up and went to the hall. The front door was wide open, but she was nowhere to be seen. He rang her. "Where are you love, did you just come back to the house for something?" Laura was in the village and no, she hadn't gone back to the house. Then he heard a bang in the bathroom, he bolted up the stairs, no one there, then he heard the front door slam. "What the....." he was downstairs in a flash and out of the front door. Jay shouted at the top of his voice into

165

the air. "Leave us alone you freak, I will bloody kill you when I get my hands on you!" Just as those words left his lips, a blast of ice-cold air hit his him with force in the face and the intense smell of gunshot filled his nostrils. He felt his lungs fill with freezing air and he fell to his knees clutching his throat. He couldn't breathe; he couldn't pull the air into his lungs. Help, he tried to call out, but there was no sound. He could feel icy fingers wrap around his throat and then nothing, just darkness, silence, black.

It didn't take Laura long to get to the village church, as it was a stone's throw from the pub. It was a beautiful, typical country village church. There were quite a few very old stones and some from the past couple of decades too. In the far-right corner near to the gate she found him.

In Loving Memory of

Peter Marsh

1932 – 1954

Our Only Son

Taken Into Gods Care Too Soon

KEEPER'S COTTAGE

Forever followed by faithful paws 🐾

SHE SAT by his stone and talked quietly to him and hoped he would listen. "We love your cottage, we want to make it our forever home. We aren't going to change it much, just enough to make sure it stands for another few hundred years. I know you are here Peter, show me how I can help you. I only know a little of your story and if that is true, I am so sorry for what happened to you. I can see if I could meet Jane and talk to her. Would that help"? As she spoke, Harvey started to get excited, tail wagging and yipping just like the greeting he gave people he liked. "I am taking that as a yes Peter, I have no idea what I will say, but I will try." At that she got up and headed back home.

As she walked up the path to the front door, she saw Jays hammer lying on the path, and picking it up she walked in, and found him sitting at the kitchen table. He looked physically shaken. "Whatever is wrong love?" Having explained what happened and the fact he thought he had blacked out, Laura insisted they see a doctor.

"I don't need a doctor, I need to find that bloody

stalker and sort him out," Jay was angry now, and got up to put on his coat. "Come on love, I am not leaving you here alone. We are going to see Martin and tell him his mate is taking this joke too bloody far."

The meeting with Martin did nothing but create an even more tense situation. Martin had sworn on his life that there was no prank, and he even offered to help them look for this man. "Honestly, we would never do such a thing, you are here every day, and we have become friends, surely?" Jay calmed down and asked Martin to spread the word to keep an eye out for this stalker, as he was now calling him.

The next day, Jay had to go for a meeting at the school, he was starting in two weeks. "Come with me and you can shop, I'll only be a few hours."

"I'm volunteering at Jane and Sarah's charity coffee thing this afternoon, remember?" Laura pulled her hair into a stubby tail. "And going shopping won't move us forward on this renovation. I am not going to let your newfound fear of my being at the cottage alone keep me from my home. We talked about this, ghost or real he means no harm to me"

Laura heard him out. Then, she simply shook her head and told him that he was being ridiculous. Besides, even if Jay was right, there had been no actual sighting of the stranger or his canine companions in nearly a week. If there was any chance at all that the man had survived the flood, surely, he had gained a better perspective on his life after being swept away. Sneaking into a locked cottage to play pranks on the new owners seemed very unlikely. They hadn't left so much as a footprint. Without some sort of proof that someone other than Jay and Laura was lurking around the cottage, there was little they could do but admit that their nerves were frayed, and the stress of the renovation was making them both feel on edge.

"Laura..." Sitting at their breakfast in the inn's large dining room, Jay knew he couldn't sway her.

"Go to work, Jay," Laura reached across the table and curled her hand around his. "I'll be fine. You need to stop worrying so much."

"Has the plumber called back yet?" Jay asked.

All of the rescheduling did nothing for his peace of mind. First, the plumber failed to arrive. Then the electrician had to reschedule. Technically, both missed visits proved to be a godsend since everything Jay touched kept going wrong. Laura, on the other hand, was sailing through her part as if some guardian angel perched on her shoulder. While Jay's tools went missing at every turn, Laura barely had to reach for hers. The wall in the bath hardly cracked no matter how many times Jay hit it but came crumbling down almost as soon as Laura aimed her hammer in its general direction. There were so many holes in the walls from Jay's attempts to trace the wiring that his darling wife had finally suggested they stop considering repair work and just start fresh.

"He is booked for the next week and a half but promised to get back to me. He still swears there was a call to cancel his original visit although, of course, he can't remember the name of the caller," Laura held up a hand to stop Jay from bringing up the idea of a stalker again. She had heard far more of that nonsense than she was comfortable with.

"The new tiles should be in today," Jay latched on to his last argument that might keep Laura away from the cottage when he wasn't there. "You could make a day of it in the village before your volunteer work. Maybe -"

"Maybe I could pick up the tiles after I help with the charity coffee as I planned so I can enjoy the fresh autumn air while it's still warm enough to open the windows at the cottage," Laura interrupted. "And maybe, you should get moving instead of trying to talk me out of going to our new home without your unnecessary supervision. You're going to be late."

Half an hour later, Laura had to admit that maybe Jay had a point about someone else gaining access to the cottage without them knowing. She had locked the door herself when they left the night before but there it was hanging open again. Cautiously, she searched the area for any hint of movement. There was none.

"I don't know who you are, but this needs to end, and it needs to end now," she said loud enough that anyone on the property might hear. "You may think you are just having a bit of fun, but the police will have a very different opinion on the matter. I fully intend to call them as soon as I go inside unless you show yourself now and apologize."

It was a risk, and Jay would be horrified if he knew she had taken it. Laura was 5 foot nothing, and slim. Jay described her as dainty although it made her feel like some fragile tea set when they both knew she was capable enough when it came to pulling her weight. The possibility of a physical fight was something completely different. Supposing Jay had a valid point about one of their neighbours taking too much interest in her, it would be best to not find out what happened when their misguided affections were not returned.

She should go back to the inn or down to the village as Jay had suggested. She knew she should. It was the safest thing to do. At the very least, she should call in reinforcements.

Laura saw Jay's hammer lying beside the door and squared her shoulders. He had spent ages looking for it last night. There was no reason for the thing to be outside and less for it to be in plain sight when she knew full well it wasn't there when they went back to the inn. That was enough to tip her caution out of the way as anger replaced her misgivings.

"If you think we are going to be run out of our home, you are devastatingly wrong," Laura declared as she stomped up to the porch and wrapped her fingers around the handle. "If you think that I am the least bit afraid of you, think again. If I ever find out who you are, rest assured that you will pay dearly for your petty antics. Jay and I are not going to be driven from our home by the likes of you. We are finished putting up with your childish behaviour."

"You are getting as bad as Jay," she told herself as she forced her shoulders to relax and her grip to loosen on the wooden handle of the hammer. "The next thing you know, you'll be losing your tools and misplacing your coffee. Speaking of which, maybe you should cut back on the caffeine. I mean, look at you, Laura. You're talking to yourself half expecting a different voice to answer. Get a grip, woman."

Blowing out a breath, Laura focused on calming down. Her heartbeat still pounded in her ears. Goosebumps rippled along her skin from both the impossible chill in the air and horror at her angry dive into what could have been a very dangerous situation. And for what? A door that had a habit of falling open? A half-seen shadow? Noises that were most likely due to an old stone cottage hunkering down over a weather change. She had let Jay's worry get to her. That was all it could be. Her future home was still the same disaster zone it had been yesterday. Nothing had changed. No boogeyman waited to pounce on her as soon as she let her guard down. She had simply let her imagination get the better of her. That was all. In that moment her thoughts turned to Peter. What if it was Peter still in his cottage and they were seeing glimpses of him, what?

She jumped when the kettle whistled, then laughed. The silliness of her reaction to such a commonplace sound finally broke through the last vestiges of wariness. Everything had a perfectly logical explanation. None even needed some stalker that Jay had conjured to fulfil them or a ghost.

Pouring her tea and putting the chamomile back in the cupboard where it should have been all along, she made another round through the cottage. This time, it was to open the windows wide so the fresh air would drive out the acrid scent of black powder lingering there. It had to have something to do with the plaster. Their only exposure to the scent had been during fireworks celebrations. Somehow, the dust in the cottage must be similar in its aroma. The little house had belonged to numerous gamekeepers over the years after all. Surely, gunpowder residue was a hazard of the job that could soak into a place. Once it was cleared, they would never have to smell it again.

As she walked back to the bathroom, Harvey's red ball rolled from the living room corner where it had been forgotten and bumped against her foot. Laura stood still for a long moment as a swirl of cold air wrapped around her legs before sliding away. She closed her eyes and counted to ten willing her heart to settle down once more.

"Perfectly logical explanation," she muttered.

"Old floors put off kilter by the weather and the fact that Jay has torn up half of their mates."

Of course that was it. There was obviously no unwanted suitor seeking her attention in the empty corner. Just a draft like all the others floating through the house. It must have gained momentum from the light breeze coming in the windows and sent Harvey's toy across the room. Laura set her tea on the nearest box and retrieved the ball. She would have to remember to take it with her when she left. The poor terrier would be happy to have it back.

She set the ball on the counter in the kitchen and went to retrieve her tea as she tried to remember where she had last left the broom. The morning was getting away from her. The charity coffee afternoon was scheduled for three o'clock, and it was nearly eleven already. She had wasted so much time that she would be lucky if she could get the old tiles from the bath boxed up and tucked away before she needed to walk back to the inn for a shower and decent clothes.

It took her fifteen minutes, but she finally found the broom leaning against the kitchen counter by the stove. She could have sworn that it wasn't there when she made her tea. Crossing her arms over her chest, she stared at it for a minute with a raised eyebrow trying to remember when she had moved it. When she couldn't immediately conjure up the memory, she drummed her short fingernails on the butcher block counter and stared at the broom some more. Finally, with a whispered curse, she grabbed the thing and carried it, along with the dustpan that was miraculously in sight atop a box labelled dishes that was on the table and made her way to the bathroom.

Everything was just as she had left it. Its thick coating of plaster was now nothing more than rubble on the floor. The tiles Laura had removed from the rest of the walls and the floor would be in neat piles inside the claw-foot tub. No footprints marred the pristine disaster of the room. Not even hers or Jay's. Too much dust had hung in the air when they were finished pulling down the interior wall where the strange knocking persisted from time to time even though they had found no plumbing to explain it. Now that the dust had settled, it coated every square inch of the space. It dusted the fixtures and sat like snow on the edge of the tub. Since the linen closet was out in the hall, Laura hadn't done more in her initial rampaging search than poke her head through the door and ensure that no one was hiding there.

As she considered the task ahead, Laura was again tempted to just leave the cottage for another day. Jay would understand even if she left out her temper tantrum at the start. It would be to everyone's benefit if she put that behind her and didn't say a word about it to her darling husband, anyway. Unfortunately, leaving now meant that the mess would be waiting the next time she walked into the cottage. Laura doubted that her motivation to clean it would be any higher then than now. Plus, the sooner it was done, the sooner she could get to cleaning the rest of the rooms. No electrician or plumber in their right mind would want to work in the kind of conditions she saw before her.

Tugging a clean dust mask into place, Laura set to work. She very much wished she knew the name of the tune that she found herself humming halfway through the job. When she tried to remember where she heard it, she came up as blank as she had when she found the broom earlier. It was pretty. Something from a bygone age, she thought, although she couldn't place it. Still, it kept her company as she scooped plaster bits into the bin and swept the dust

Laura checked her watch and found that she would have just enough time to take a short break if she wanted to finish and box up the tiles before she left. Once again, she found her mug sitting beside the box of tea on the counter and shook her head. Hadn't she put both where they belonged? It was a small thing but it rattled her more than she liked, especially since she needed to be on her game when she went to the charity coffee. The funds being raised were for a garden project that Laura desperately wanted to be involved in. Everything about her time in the cottage this morning made her feel off-kilter.

She made herself another cup of tea and stepped outside into the fresh air to enjoy it. That was what she needed to clear the dust and cobwebs out of her head. The day was so pretty, too. Absently, Laura imagined how her home would look at this time next year. There would be a riot of flowers to brighten things up, then. And a nice little pool lined with the old olive-green tiles to reflect all of the colours. The interior would be finished. The property transformed from its current bedraggled state into something truly beautiful. Just the thought renewed her determination to get through the ugly stage of the renovation now.

As she turned to go back inside, Laura heard a crash from the bathroom. She set out at a run with thoughts of the ceiling raining down to shatter against the newly cleaned floor racing around her mind. When she reached the door, everything looked just as it had when she stepped away. She took a cautious step toward the tub, all the while scanning the ceiling for some chunk of fallen plaster that she had somehow missed. There was nothing else it could have been. When she reached the tub, she found it dust-free and shining as if scrubbed clean. Stranger, the handle of Jay's hammer - the same hammer she knew she had left in the office where it would be needed next - stood straight up in the centre of the sparkling porcelain. Beneath it, olive green tiles lay shattered in the shape of a heart.

A chill raced up Laura's spine. No amount of rationally explaining to herself that there was an explanation at hand if she only looked for it untied the knot twisting in her stomach. When frigid air enveloped her, causing her breath to fog visibly as it puffed out in short, panicked gasps, Laura ran.

It wasn't until halfway back to the inn that she calmed down enough to force herself to stop. The windows were still open. The door, too. She couldn't leave the cottage like that. Not just because some childish fear had gripped her. Swallowing although her mouth had gone dry, Laura turned back. If she inched up to the cottage door, she still forced herself to go through it. She closed and locked the windows, even the one in the tiny bathroom where the heart of shattered tiles still lay glistening in the old bathtub.

"This is my house. My home. Jay and I are going to build our future here together," tears choked Laura's declaration. She wanted so badly to find the anger that had engulfed her when she first arrived. Instead, her heart felt broken. It was all too much to bear. The beautiful cottage of her dreams was quickly turning into a nightmare. "Peter, if this is you trying to haunt us out of your cottage please please stop. We mean you no harm, we love your cottage, but we want to make it ours" Laura put her hand to her head, she was now talking to ghosts.

Harvey's ball sat on a small table just inside the door. It didn't matter if she thought she had left it on the kitchen counter. Laura picked it up, ignoring the way her hand shook as she did so, and slipped it into her pocket. She closed the door firmly and made sure the lock slid into place. Then, walking on legs that felt too rubbery for a grown woman faced with nothing more threatening than broken ceramics, Laura made her way back to the inn.

She wouldn't speak of this, she told herself firmly. Not to Jay. Not to anyone. If, at some point, she found some explanation that made any sense at all, then she might gloss over some rendition of the past few hours. Not now. Not when her eyes stung with tears she couldn't explain either. Not when her heart felt so very heavy for no logical reason. Fear, she could have rationalized away. She could have laughed in the face of it now that the moment had passed and she was walking beneath the autumn sun. Not this heaviness sitting on her soul like a mountain.

There was still the charity coffee to consider. It wasn't until Laura was out of a long, hot shower that she made up her mind not to cancel. She needed a piece of normality right now nearly as much as she needed the hours to hurry by and bring Jay back to her. If she closeted herself away at the inn, there would be far too much time for her mind to race as she tried to make sense of the morning. So, she did her best to shed concerns over the cottage as she got dressed and put on her makeup. She wanted to meet people in the village, and this was a good way to do it.

Only a few people were out along the riverwalk as she made her way into the village. Some sat on the benches enjoying their lunch and tossing an occasional crust of bread to the ducks that called the riverbank their home. Laura breathed a sigh of relief. After the morning she'd had, seeing that the world went on as it always did, helped to ground her.

Then, as if Fate had been waiting for just the right moment when Laura's guard was down, she saw him. The old-fashioned cap covered his hair as it always did. An earthtone vest with deep pockets stretched across his broad shoulders. The sleeves of his shirt were rolled to the elbows. He walked with a confident gate as if he knew his place in the world and nothing could dislodge him from it. Two black dogs trotted at his side. He turned from across the riverbank and waved with a big wide handsome smile, she waved frantically back, and without thinking she called his name. "Peter, wait, come back!"

But he carried on walking.

Laura gasped. There was no way it could be the same man that had been swept away in the flood waters. Yet, she knew it was. There was no doubt in her mind. Her feet raced over the hard ground as she hurried to catch up to him. He was heading back toward the Footpaths, pausing now and then to toss something into the water for the dogs to chase. It should have been easy for her to reach him, yet she couldn't. Her breath came sharp and fast. A stitch formed in her side. Still, he remained too far ahead for her to call out again. Then, as she rounded the big tree next to the river and she lost sight of him altogether.

She ran on, anyway. He couldn't have disappeared. She couldn't let him disappear. Not this time. Not when she had so many questions. But no matter how hard she looked, she couldn't find him. Finally, nearly at the edge of the woods, she gave up. He was a man as real as any, he couldn't be a ghost, from what she had seen in her google searches they were not as "real" as he was, they were shadows, faint apparitions. But she knew with every part of her being, that this was Peter.

She was still pondering his reappearance and what it meant when she arrived at the pretty little house that Jane and Sarah Noble called home. Pulling herself together and smoothing her hair, Laura walked up the short, flower-lined path and knocked on the door. She had promised Peter she would talk to Jane, but now it all seemed a bit far-fetched.

"Ah, you must be Laura. Come in," Sarah Noble, wrinkled now but still as sweet as she had always been answered the door with a delighted smile. Looking closer at Laura, her smile turned to a look of concern. "My dear, are you quite alright? You look like you have seen a ghost. Come in. Sit down for a minute. You are far too pale. Jane? Bring us a cup of tea if you would."

"I'm fine," Laura assured her. "I've just had a trying morning, and it seems to be catching up to me all at once. Please, don't go to any trouble. I'm supposed to be helping you today, not the other way around."

"Nonsense," Jane, white-haired now but still full of the same wild spirit she had in her youth, said as she came from the kitchen with a cup in her hand. "If Sarah says you need to sit down and drink this, that is exactly what you need to do. She always knows. You might as well tell her outright what the problem is, too. She'll ferret it out of you if you don't."

"It's nothing," Laura found her elbow in Sarah's gentle but insistent grip as she was led to a chair in the dining room. "Really. I just saw someone along the river who shocked me. My husband and I believed he had been carried away in the flood. While I am very relieved to find this isn't the case, seeing him and his dogs after a morning full of oddities at our new cottage has me feeling a bit unsettled. I'll be fine in a minute."

"Oh!" Jane said with a bright smile, although she was watching Laura just as closely as her sister. The last time she had seen someone as pale as the woman sitting at the table was now, there had been a nasty fainting spell involved. "You and your husband are the ones who bought my cottage. I thought as much when I heard your name. I was hoping to meet you. Christine didn't mention that when she said you would like to volunteer today, so I wasn't sure."

"That is completely my fault," Laura shook her head. "I'm afraid that I asked her not to. I didn't want you to think that I was only coming today to meet the previous owner. Now, I'm afraid I've managed to make a bad first impression on top of it. Please, accept my apology."

"Goodness," Sarah laughed. Now that Laura had some colour back, she wasn't nearly as worried. "Even if that was your main reason for coming to help, Jane and I are both smart enough to accept the offer anyway. These charity coffees are more than our old hands can handle on their own anymore. Now, you finish that tea and tell us about your morning. We have plenty of time. Our guest won't be arriving for an hour yet, and we can talk while we set out the China and brew the coffee."

"It seems silly now," Laura cringed. Now that she had made a solid fool of herself in front of the ladies, she didn't want to add to it with an explanation that was anything but rational.

"I've heard that you and your husband are making some changes to the cottage," Jane eased herself into the chair across from Laura. "If you are worried that I might be bothered about that, rest assured that I am not. It should be a home again. I kept it to myself for far too long. Now that it belongs to you, it should reflect who you are, not remain the memory I was holding on to so tightly."

"I didn't want to change it all at once," Laura felt tears stinging her eyes again. She took a sip of tea to wash the heartache down. "Jay didn't either. We wanted small changes over time so we could grow into the cottage and it could grow around us. Now, here we are ripping it to pieces with no end in sight and no clue as to why the problems we are chasing exist. Jay believes that someone is causing trouble. Possibly even sneaking in when we aren't looking. I thought he was imagining some of it but this morning was so strange that I can't help but believe he may be right."

"What type of problems?" Jane looked appalled.

KEEPER'S COTTAGE

"I insisted that the cottage be kept up. If I find out it wasn't"

"That's just it," Laura interrupted shaking her head emphatically. "It was. We have found absolutely nothing wrong no matter how hard we have looked. We are still waiting on the plumber and the electrician to verify that, but everything looks like it is in perfect order. It's the most maddening part of it all - or nearly so."

Laura set the dainty cup down and sighed. How was she ever going to explain it to them when she didn't even understand what was going on herself.

CHAPTER

NINE

1954

Jane barely noticed the months slipping away. They held no interest for her now that Peter was gone. Nothing did.

The village doctor sent her into a drug-induced sleep once he knew for certain there was nothing he could do for the man covered in a sheet at the estate's side garden. Jane's hysteria made it so she could barely breathe. Everyone in the house did their best to calm her but there was no other recourse. Her consciousness swam through it as the people of Adington came together to pack away the decorations and booths. Many of them whispered about the events as they did or cast furtive eyes at the windows of the big house. Enough had overhead

Jane's screaming accusation to wonder why John Noble was allowed the comfort of his own chair as the police questioned him on the matter. Many knew Peter well enough to put the pieces together and see how he and Jane might have been in the middle of a secret affair. That turned to talk about how well-matched they were and a newfound sympathy for a girl that, until that moment, had been seen with affectionate amusement. By the time the last booth was quietly removed from the lawn, they were sure that they knew the truth of things. They were also angry. The Noble's gamekeeper was a good friend, a hard worker, and someone any father should have been happy to see his daughter take an interest in.

That cast her father in a much different light than the one they were used to seeing him in. The more he tried to gain their support by repeating how the shooting was an accident, the less they believed him. When he began hinting that Peter should have known better than to stand where he was, they turned against John Noble entirely.

Sally, once the most vibrant thing at her parents' bakery, couldn't meet anyone's eye when she stood at the counter. She fell silent, subdued by some inner demon that made her face pale and her hands shake. Within a month, she was sent to live with relatives far from Adington and the rumours flew again. Less so, this time, and with more sympathy than anger, but they flew all the same. Before talk of her jealousy faded, her parents closed the bakery and followed their daughter to a new life far from the village they had called home.

When Jane was finally allowed to wake, she, too was quiet. She ate when Sarah brought her a tray and told her to eat. She bathed when Sarah drew her bath and sat beside the tub to wash her hair. The rest of Jane's time was spent staring out at the snow when it fell. Grief stole her days and haunted her nights.

Christmas came and went. The old year died and was reborn. A few well-meaning visitors to the house tried to dispel the gloom but none stayed long. Somehow, the walls themselves reverberated with the girl's anguish and her father's solemn gloom. There would be a police inquiry, it seemed. One that John Noble had not expected. Nor had he expected that his daughters would turn against him so completely. Even Sarah was distant and overly formal with him now. She chose to spend her days reading of ways to pull Jane from her misery or sitting at her sister's side willing her to come away from the shadow that locked Jane away in a personal hell.

Peter's absence was a physical pain too deep to allow Jane's tears to fall. Sometimes, when she was blessedly alone, she whispered to him of the life they would have had. She dreamed that she was by his side, the echo of happiness ringing hollow once her eyes fluttered open on a new day that he would never see. She wondered how the world could still exist without him, how she could still be flesh and blood when her heart had gone with him to his grave. Surely, it was impossible. She begged the heavens to correct their mistake by giving Peter back to her or at least ending her misery so she could find him in what lay beyond her last breath.

Sarah came every day to read to her or tell her about the day's events. Jane knew she meant well. Somewhere inside, Jane understood that still. She just didn't care anymore. Not even when Sarah broke the news that Peter's shooting had been ruled an accident. It came as no surprise. Nor did it add to the hopelessness she existed in now.

Jane didn't bother reading the report that her sister left on her bedside table. She already knew what it would say. John Noble was a respected member of the peerage. He was a good and decent man. There had never been even the smallest hint of violence in him. No one would ever believe him capable of murder. Because they could not believe that he had become a monster, the shooting had to be an accident as he claimed. She cast the pages into the fire as soon as Sarah left the room.

Jane knew the truth of John Noble's *accidental* shooting of his gamekeeper. She would always know the truth. So did the man who had raised her. No lie, no matter how official it was could ever fill the chasm between them. The man she once called Father was as dead to her as Peter. Jane refused to be in the same room with him. The one time he tried to speak to her, Sarah had to call the doctor to have her sedated. Since then, Jane had stayed in her room letting the world spin around her and the monster who had killed her lover had kept to his own shadows. As far as Jane was concerned, her father was gone. He had succumbed to an illness of the mind that caused him to become something vile. Let him haunt his house as he chose so long as he did not ever again try to invade the fragile bubble of the life he had left her with.

When spring came, Jane finally stepped foot out of her room. Everyone had stopped watching for her to do something rash. They saw her as a broken doll that sat silently at the window. They believed she was no more capable of harming herself than she was of finding joy in the treats they brought her. Even the doctor who occasionally came to peer into her eyes and listen to the beat of her shattered heart deemed her safe enough to be left unattended. At one point he had suggested that Jane be institutionalized until she was well once more. Sarah was the one to stand in the way of that horror. Now, even she believed the day would never come when Jane would be herself again.

The moon hung bright enough to make Jane put up a shielding hand as she slipped out the back door and waded into the thick fog rolling in from the river. Ghostly visitations. She had thought that old wives' tale was funny once. Now, she hoped with all her heart it was true. If so, Peter might take her hand in the mist. He might make her whole again. If not, perhaps she could follow him beyond this life. Maybe there, they could finally find the happiness that should have been their right.

She curled up on the cottage stoop when she reached it. Fog enveloped her, blocking out the moonlight along with the world she so desperately wanted to escape. The first tears she had managed since the night Peter died rolled down her cheeks.

"Please find me," Jane whispered. "I'm so lost without you, Peter."

Warmth wrapped around her as his arms once had. She closed her eyes and burrowed into it as if he held her. Sobbing, she drifted off to sleep.

When the first rays of dawn stretched across the sky, Jane awoke feeling better than she had in months. Duke and Squire stood like sentries beside her. For the first time, she thought that maybe she could go on. If not for her own sake, she could do it for Peter. The life John Noble had stolen from him could live on through her. Peter deserved that much. In her heart, she knew that he would want her happy. The pain that had swallowed her would have broken his heart. She was the cause of far too much misery already. She had to find a way to turn her life into something that would make him proud.

"Jane?" Sarah let her shock show when Jane stepped into the kitchen. "You're up? And you're dressed? Where...how...never mind. It doesn't matter. It's just so good to see you out of your room."

"Yes," Jane attempted a smile. After slipping back into the house, she had taken a long, hot bath, combed the tangles out of her hair, and gotten dressed. She needed a belt and her shirt felt baggy.

There were dark crescents beneath her eyes. She accepted her appearance for what it was and knew that as she healed, it would improve. She brushed away Sarah's worried perusal with a flick of her hand. "It took me a while, but I'm ready to face things. I might need a little help here and there but I'm ready to start at least. Where is he?"

"Father?" Sarah asked. There was no one else that it could be but Jane understood the need for clarification. She had called out to Peter so many times that Sarah must think she believed he might answer.

"I'll never call him that again." Jane raised her chin slightly.

"He went to London a few weeks ago. Richard suggested it," Sarah chose her words carefully.

"After the ruling," Jane nodded. "I remember now."

"Are you..." Sarah didn't finish the question.

"Alright?" Jane supplied. "Not yet, but I will be. This is just the starting point. I have a long way to go. Is there tea? And breakfast. I believe I'm hungry."

Sarah watched her a little too closely but that was to be expected after what Jane knew she had put the girl through. What mattered was that Jane knew that she was going to be okay. Her sister would understand that truth soon enough.

"Have you been handling the estate all on your own?" Jane asked feeling suddenly guilty. Grief was a self-indulgent thing. It couldn't help being so any more than Jane could have stopped herself from sinking into it. Sarah never should have had it all put on her shoulders.

"Richard has been helping." Sarah's cheeks turned a pretty pink.

"Tell me he's had the good sense to see just how wonderful you are, Sarah," Jane said sincerely. Sarah deserved so much in life. She deserved as much love as the world had to offer and more. "It would make me very happy to hear that he has. I told him when we first met that the two of you had a lot in common. He's a good man. One nearly deserving of your heart."

"I don't think..." Sarah stammered. "Jane, you've only now left your room. Please don't make me worry more than I already am."

"I'm still mourning, Sarah," Jane admitted. "I will always be mourning Peter in one way or another. I'm dealing with the loss of my father, as well. I know that now. I understand my grief. I understand the time it will take and that there will be bad days to come when it feels like my sadness might drown me again. I accept that. I'll live for Peter on those days. I will find joy for him if I can't find it for myself. I owe him that, Sarah. None of this would have happened if I hadn't let myself love him or convinced him that he loved me, too. Maybe he would have gone his whole life and never seen me as anyone more important than the boss's pest of a daughter if I had left well enough alone." She shook her head sadly when Sarah tried to argue. "I have to own my part of this whole horrible mess. If I don't, I will never be able to forgive myself. I need to do that for Peter's sake if for no other reason. And I owe you thanks that I haven't given you yet. So much more than just thanks. You pulled me through to this moment. I am grateful and so very happy to have you as my sister. If you tell me that you have a chance at love, I will be more so."

Sarah had her arms around Jane as soon as the words were out. She was crying nearly as hard as Jane had the night before. They were happy tears this time, filled with joy and hope and so many words that it took Sarah the rest of the day to say them. By the time they fell asleep in front of the fireplace like they had when they were girls, Sarah had finally gotten around to admitting that she wanted nothing more than to give her heart to Richard but wasn't sure he felt the same.

Two weeks later, they both got their answer when Richard proposed. This time it was to Sarah. Jane could feel the love radiating off of the couple like the sun that burned bright in the nearly cloudless sky overhead. It gave her a new kind of peace.

"Sarah and I have been talking," Richard took Sarah's hand as they all sat together on the porch one evening just after the quiet ceremony that made them man and wife. Adington had rejoiced at the announcement but respected the couple's decision to keep the celebration small and intimate. At Sarah's insistence, Richard's father had given her away while his mother and Jane stood as witnesses. After that, the small party held a dinner for the town but slipped away before the dancing started. Richard's parents were leaving the next day to travel. Their dreams of building up the estate had soured. "This place isn't good for you. There are too many memories here. I will be taking over my parents' estate now that they have gone off on their new adventure. Sarah will finish moving her things over the next few weeks. We would like you to do the same and come to live with us. This isn't just because we worry about you. We could use the help.

We have so many plans that our two hands can't handle them alone. You could make a new home there and build a life without anyone telling you that you have to be someone you're not. We would promise that and see that the promise is kept."

"What about this estate?" Jane looked around. The familiar stone walls of the estate where she had lived all her life were nothing more than a childish attempt to recreate the home it once was to her. "Will *he* come back to live here?"

"No," Richard shifted beside Sarah, as there was more news that needed to be broken. So long as none of it involved her having to see John Noble again, Jane had nothing to fear from it. "The current plan is to sell the estate and put the money in a trust for you and Sarah. The people of Adington accept the verdict that was handed down on the surface, but they have also seen far too much of the aftermath to not question it in their hearts. They turned their backs on John long before he went to London and he knows it. He won't be returning. You and Sarah could demand that the estate be put into your names rather than sold. I don't believe he would fight that. You could remain here if that is what you want, although I hope you reconsider."

"I don't think you should stay in this house,"

Sarah chimed in. "Not by yourself. Not after what happened. Even I feel the difference in it now. There are too many shadows. All the happiness we had growing up is gone. This is no longer our home, Jane. It is just a place where something horrible happened. I don't think you should continue living here."

"I want the cottage," Jane held up a hand before anyone could interrupt. "Not to live in. I don't think I could bear it without Peter. I want it cut from the estate as was promised. I want the forest behind it with the Footpaths that Peter walked with Duke and Squire every day. I will, of course, be keeping the dogs, as well. Not the pheasants. Those, I want to go somewhere that they will be taken care of. It makes me sick to think they could meet their end the same way that Peter did after he took so much care raising them and keeping them healthy. I know it's silly. I don't mind that. I just need to know that they can live out their lives safe from foxes and rifles. I need to know that they will be fed and given clean water. If at all possible, I want them to go somewhere that their new keepers will talk to them and tell them how beautiful they are just as Peter did. I want the place that Peter called home kept up and taken care of. Someday, perhaps, I will be able to let it go. Until then, I will leave it to you, Richard, to decide how best to handle it. As long as the cottage and the land it comes with hold true to their bones, I will have no complaints. I may visit from time to time but I will not interfere otherwise. I want nothing else from this estate or from the man who owns it. If you will allow me to have a place in your home, that is more than enough of a future for me. Do what you will with the rest of whatever comes into my name. I have no desire to touch it. We will have papers drawn up if that makes everything easier."

"Jane, you may meet someone -" Richard cringed at the look his sister-in-law gave him and stopped short.

"There will be no one else, Richard," Jane informed him softly. He had to know the truth upfront. "I gave my heart to Peter. The rest of my life is his as much as mine. There will be no one else. Know that before you open your home to me. I won't leave until they carry me away from my deathbed. Until then, I will do my best to make Sarah's efforts to preserve my life meaningful. I will help care for your home and any children you may have. I would like to have some purpose there that takes me back into nature as well. I've been cooped up for far too long. Help me find it and I will be content."

Richard eventually agreed but only so far as the cottage and land were concerned. He insisted she keep control of the remainder of her trust. Jane made a game of finding ways to spend the money from it to better her new home and spoil her four nieces and nephews as they came along.

Jane found happiness once more in her new life. She kept true to herself while helping Sarah run the household and providing Richard with inspiration for the grounds. For a time, the social circle that was so important to her father tried to draw her close. They invited her to parties. Jane always sent her regrets politely but firmly. The eligible bachelors hinted at courting her. Each time, Jane rebuffed their attempts to pull her into a world that held no meaning for her. Eventually, she was left to the new peace she had discovered. Jane loved her family. She loved the life she shared with them. It was enough.

Sarah laughingly complained that Jane had become the wild aunt who showed the children all the ways they could get up to mischief. Jane argued that mischief was in the eye of the beholder and that she was merely making sure that they understood all that nature had to offer. If it meant they came in covered in mud, all the better. By the time they were grown, all four were as well-rounded and capable as their father, as loving as their mother, as unconventional as their aunt, and, Jane thought, as marvellous as Peter. It was a good combination and they prospered from it.

There were days when Jane still struggled. When Duke grew grey in the muzzle and slipped away in his sleep. Then when Squire followed a few weeks later. They were the last breathing ties to Peter that Jane had. She buried them in the clearing where they once chased foxes and retrieved pheasants for those who hunted them. The bench she had placed at their graves became a new favourite place to think when the world felt too heavy. She felt the dogs there, Peter as well. If she sat quietly enough, she could almost convince herself that she heard them all in the rustle of the leaves overhead.

The morning that news came that John Noble was dead, Jane went to the bench and sat until long after the sun sank below the trees and the crickets began their song. She hadn't talked to him in almost two decades. She was nearly as old as the father she once loved had been when he became the monster that killed Peter. Her dark hair was threaded with silver. Her knees ached when she climbed the steps to her room. Her face showed the map of a life spent outdoors instead of the smooth skin that Peter had so loved to touch.

To her surprise, she cried more than once that day. Tears flowed for the father she had lost so long ago and for the events that had ripped him from her life. Not just hers, but Sarah's life as well. And the children that Sarah had brought into the world who had never even met their grandfather. They had never known what it was like to be greeted with his kiss on the top of their heads when he came to breakfast. They had never heard his deep, boisterous laugh or had him read them a bedtime story on a rainy night. One horrific afternoon so long ago that Jane sometimes feared she might forget some small detail of the moments before everything went wrong stole that from them. It broke her heart all over again.

A letter arrived the following day. In it, John admitted what he had done. He begged Jane's forgiveness although he said he did not believe she owed it to him. He had never found peace with his actions. For years, he had wrestled with the knowledge that he had acted rashly and the consequences were a weight he carried until his final day. He knew he could never make things right again. Not for

Peter. Not for Jane. Not even for himself. Still, he hoped that she might remember who he was before that day fondly. In the end, John Noble asked his daughter for one final thing. He wished to be buried in Adington.

Jane and Sarah gave him his wish although neither of them attended the funeral. The father they had known had been gone for a lifetime at that point. The empty shell in its pine box had little to do with them. They chose a headstone to mark his grave for the sake of the father they once loved but that was as far as either sister was willing to go. It wasn't until years later that they even saw it.

When Richard became ill two years after his last daughter married and left the family home to build her life with a small-town doctor, Jane took turns with Sarah watching over him. As grief descended on her home once more, it was Jane who helped Sarah find a way through it. She carried trays to her sister's bedside and read to her to encourage Sarah to eat. She drew baths and sat beside the big claw-foot tub to wash Sarah's hair. They sat in silence long into the night until Sarah could find her words again. Then, they walked the gardens until Sarah was strong enough for Jane to take her out to Richard's favourite places.

Jane understood the peace those spots held. She did everything in her power to ensure that Sarah spent time in each one just as Jane spent time at Peter's cottage when the day felt heavy or she needed to feel like she was near him. Neither sister ever really escaped their sadness, but they did learn to live with it and draw from the deep well of it to savour the joy that came their way all the more.

In time, the sisters turned the running of the estate over to Sarah's children and focused on giving back to the people of Adington in other ways. The village had grown over the years although it was still small enough to retain its charm. New faces appeared and took the place of those who moved away. New dreams formed as those of the past were turned into reality. Jane and Sarah embraced the magic of it all with such enthusiasm that any cause they took up was sure to succeed.

As they grew older, that enthusiasm never waned. They did, however, finally agree to confine their efforts to hosting a monthly charity coffee morning to raise funds for the various projects and opportunities Adington had to offer. It was fulfilling work that drew the community together. Under Jane and Sarah's watchful eyes, the village thrived. This, too, led to growth and more new faces.

Peter, gone so much longer now than the years he had lived, would have been proud. Jane was sure of it. That, and the love that surrounded her was far more than enough to make Jane content in the twilight years of her life. One day before too much more time passed, she would join him in the great mystery that lay beyond her life. She had no doubt he would be there to greet her when that day came.

On a day in late autumn, Jane visited the cottage again. She sat on the edge of the bed they had once shared and closed her eyes. The creak of the floorboards always reminded her of his steps. The chilly air through the open window drove out any mustiness and seemed to carry the scent of his cologne. Everything had been kept exactly as Peter left it his last morning. Jane had insisted on it. It gave her comfort to see the half-read book on his bedside table and his coffee mug still in the sink. The small closet still held his clothes and the pillow where he once rested his head was still as plump as he had left it after straightening the covers.

Jane sighed softly and eased up from her seat with the aid of a cane. It was time to let the cottage become a home again. She had kept it breathless for far too long. Months passed where she could not manage the walk to visit its rooms. She would keep some of the things he had left behind, but most would be carried away by late afternoon. After that, the for-sale sign would go up and it would no longer be hers. She hoped that whoever made it their home found the love that she and Peter were forced to leave behind. There was plenty of it to go around.

Threading her arm through the basket that held the few things she could not let go of, Jane looked around one last time.

"It's time for you to start fresh, old friend," Jane said softly to the thick stone walls. "Be good to whoever finds you. Keep them safe and dry. Help them find the life that Peter and I should have had here. I'm counting on you."

After Jane closed the door for the last time, she didn't look back. She smiled as she made her slow way up the path knowing that somewhere, Peter was watching over her just as he had done every night when he thought she hadn't noticed. He would see her safely home just as he always did. And if she stumbled along the way, she still believed he would be right there to keep her from falling.

CHAPTER

TEN

Present Day

"Why don't you start at the beginning," Sarah suggested taking a seat beside her sister. "What made you believe there was a problem with the cottage in the first place?"

"There was a draft. Not just a movement of air along the floor. That would have been expected. What we are dealing with is far different. One minute, everything is fine. The next, it's as if you stepped into deep winter. Then, it's gone again." Once Laura started, the words came tumbling out. "It was so bad the first night that we ended up trading the bedroom and office because we were afraid we might never get to sleep because of the shivering. Our dog, Harvey, is...well, he acts like he is terrified to even be near the cottage. We thought at first it was just the new place with all the wildlife he had never met just outside the door. Now we think maybe he was smelling something we couldn't at first. The kitchen light flickers from time to time and there is an odd aroma, like gunpowder, that lingers in the air. It grew stronger once we started taking the tiles in the bath down and Jay pulled up a few floorboards to check the foundation. Dogs have such fine-tuned noses that a smell he is unfamiliar with in a place he isn't used to might have put him off. Jay thinks it's either coming from the wiring or possibly the plaster. And the blasted front door opens on its own even when we are sure we shut it tight and locked it. And I swear things move around when we aren't looking. I thought at first that I kept forgetting where I put them. My coffee mug, the broom, and tea that I was sure I tucked back into the cupboard. All little things that shouldn't bother me. Jay is one of the most organised people I know, and now he is always looking for his tools. It's so unlike him to misplace anything that it has me worried. We've been so busy - far busier than we expected to be. Plus, we are staying at the inn instead of the home we want so badly to settle into. The stress of it could very well have us forgetting where we left things. But then today..."

Jane was pale now, too. Her old fingers were wrapped around a silver locket over her heart. Sarah had her folded hands over her lips as she leaned forward, listening intently.

"I was cleaning up the plaster we pulled down on the bathroom wall so the plumber could look for pipes that may be knocking in the walls - which aren't in that location at all, so we created that mess for nothing...but I was cleaning up yet another piece of our chaos all the same. I stepped out to get some air and heard a crash. When I ran in, Jay's hammer was in the bathtub. I know I left it in the office. I know I did. He couldn't find it yesterday when he wanted to repair the floor. It was outside for some reason. I found it and after carrying it like some Viking Warhammer through the house because the door was standing open when I arrived, I put it in the office. But there it was in the bath anyway. Worse, some of the tiles that I had planned to use on a project in the garden were smashed under it. They looked exactly like a broken heart. And the tub was spotless. I mean, not just clean, although when I walked out, it was covered in plaster dust. It was shining. I was only outside for a few minutes. I had checked the whole house when I got there, even the crawl space. I didn't see anyone. I don't know how to explain it. I can't even explain how Harvey's ball rolled across the floor or how it ended up on the table by the door when I left it in the kitchen. I just can't explain any of it and it makes me feel like I'm going mad."

Laura covered her face with both hands. She hadn't meant to say even half of what had just come out in her rambling rant. It was mortifying. All she wanted to do was get up and leave the two lovely women before they realised, they should order her out or worse, call the police and suggest that she be taken to the clinic for an evaluation.

"I think we better postpone our meeting," Sarah said softly. "Whatever is going on at the cottage needs to be dealt with first. If someone is causing problems there, they need to be found out and punished. We owe it to our new friends to help them find the answers they need. Am I right, Jane?"

"I agree," Jane pounded a fist on the table and then smoothed the cloth she rumpled. "I will not have a place that I loved so dearly cause anyone grief. There has been far more than enough of that attached to it already. Sarah, will you make the calls? I will gather the photo albums and we can all look through them. Perhaps we will find out how this vile invader is gaining access to cause their havoc. Keep the kettle hot and find something sweet to drive off the sour taste of these shenanigans, if you would."

"I don't want you to put off the coffee. Not for me. It's such a good cause," Laura felt sick at the thought. "Please. I'll pull myself together and we will pretend I wasn't just a babbling idiot. I'm sure that the cottage will sort itself out. I've overreacted horribly and dumped it all in your laps. I should never have done that. I am so sorry. Please, don't put off the charity coffee. So many people will be let down. If I am a distraction, I can duck out after I help you set the table."

"The cause will keep. This won't," Jane insisted. "Life coming back to the cottage is something I dearly want. I will not have some good-for-nothing making that difficult. Come with me, Laura. I may need help with the albums. My memory isn't as clear as it once was. I may have forgotten something vital that they will show. If there is a hidden way into your new home, we will find it."

Laura followed Jane. No argument would stand against the old woman's determination. Whatever Laura had set in motion by sharing her story, she had the distinct impression that Jane Noble would not back down until she saw the situation set to rights. Sarah, either. Age may have stolen the strength of their bodies but their wills were as formidable as iron.

"I'm sure you have heard the stories by now," Jane touched the locket again. "The ones about me and Peter Marsh, I mean. The people of Adington are good-hearted but they do tend to love their gossip. By the time everyone is finished adding some new detail, the truth tends to get lost. It is important to me that you know that he and I loved each other very much. We were planning to run away the day he died so violently...so unnecessarily. My father...I haven't called him that in so very long. He was of a different time, you see. He had a set way of thinking. Before everything that happened, he was such a good man. A wonderful father, as well. I thought, back then, that once Peter and I escaped and built a life together, Father would eventually accept the difference in our social status. He liked Peter quite well, you know. And he loved me and Sarah more than life itself. Maybe that was what broke him. The love that Peter and I shared betrayed my father's trust so completely that some-thing in him shattered. I do not believe now that he meant to kill the man I loved. Not truly. The man who raised me never could have done such a thing."

Jane handed Laura three old photo albums before leading her back to the dining room table. She was thoughtful now. The old sadness had mellowed over the years or at least grown easier to bear. She had lost so much that fateful day, yet she had found a way to build a future on the wreckage.

"I wish I knew what to say to you, Jane. The only thing I can do is offer my apologies for bringing such terrible memories back again today," Laura wished she had stayed at the inn. This new turn of events only made her already miserable day that much worse. To know that she had ruined what should have been a joyful fundraising event for Sarah and Jane as well made her ashamed.

"Not only terrible memories, Laura," Jane turned to her with a sad smile. "Beautiful ones, as well. Peter and I didn't have a lifetime together but we knew more love in the time we had than some are ever blessed with. I have to forgive my father every day for what he did but I have learned to do so because of the man that he once was. I am only sorry that it took me so long after his death to figure that part out. Sarah and I lost him that day, as well, you see. She is the real hero of the story although she would tell you that she only did what needed to be done. She weathered the tragedy of it all without losing her sweetness. She pulled me through my pain and gave me a life filled with so much love that it nearly filled the emptiness that horrible day created in my life. Peter has lived on in my heart although it has been a lifetime since I held his hand in mine. As I said, I feel it is important that you know the truth. You may hear the story a hundred times in a hundred different ways. All that matters is that the story of John Noble's daughter and his gamekeeper is a love story from beginning to end."

Laura shifted the old books in her arms so she could wipe a tear away. She wished she could have known them all back then. She wished she could have somehow made the outcome far kinder.

"Jay and I, we have that kind of love," she said softly. "We have had it for nearly two decades and I hope for many more to come. I wish that life had been different for all of you."

"I do, too," Jane sighed. "But life gives us what it gives us. It's our job to make the best of it. One day soon, mine will be over and Peter will be there waiting. I feel that strongly. My father will be there, too. I like to think that once they were away from this world, they were great friends again. All the silliness of titles was behind them and they could both be just who they were: two wonderful men who loved me. Although I am in no great rush to follow them into the hereafter, I admit that I'm looking forward to finally feeling whole again when it happens."

"You have such a lovely way of looking at things, Jane," Laura wondered if she could ever show such grace.

"Age brings many things. Aches and pains, wrinkles and white hair, just to name a few. I have been lucky enough for it to bring me peace as well," her frail shoulders shrugged. "That is thanks to Sarah, Richard, and their lovely family. Now, we get to help you find a bit of it at the cottage. And if that means snaring some villain in the process, all the better. I haven't been on a good hunt in ages. I hope you don't mind if I find this one just a bit more fun than is appropriate."

"Not at all," Laura laughed at Jane's mischievous grin. All of her misgivings were gone. For the first time in weeks, Laura felt like she was in exactly the right place doing just the right thing.

"I know that look," Sarah raised an eyebrow at her sister when they all gathered around the table.

"What look is that?" Jane asked innocently.

"The one that says you are about to dive head-first into an adventure that you haven't even packed a sandwich for," Sarah sighed indulgently.

"Only from my comfortable chair and I plan to bring you right along with me," Jane grinned back. "Besides, it was your idea in the first place as I recall. And we have some lovely little cakes to enjoy while we take this walk down memory lane."

"How old are these photos?" Laura asked, carefully turning the yellowed page of the book Jane handed to her first. Black and white or shades of umber haunted the pages with faces long gone from the world. Some were faded to the point where she had to squint to make out details.

"Oh goodness," Sarah leaned closer after settling her glasses into place. "Those are far older than Jane and I. They should be in date order or at least as close as we could guess when we put the books together. I believe some of this first book may date back to the mid-eighteen hundreds. We Nobles have always loved a good photograph. See there? You can just make out the cottage at the corner of the picture. I believe I have a painting tucked away somewhere that shows it as well. And, if all else fails, we can call my grandson and have him see if the blueprints are in one of the trunks in the attic."

"The village hasn't changed much, has it?" Jane

rubbed the silver locket with the pad of her thumb as she studied the pictures. "The faces have, of course, but the buildings are nearly identical to what they were all that time ago. Ah, there's the cottage from a different angle. Hmmm. I half expected to see some sort of root cellar tucked away but so far nothing. We'll keep looking. I know the answer is here somewhere."

"Jay would love these!" Laura couldn't help but drink in the old images. She knew she should be focusing mainly on the cottage but there was so much to see. The estate was in its prime in the older pictures. It stood as stately and imposing as the finest gentleman of the day. Its gardens flourished. The village, too. Even without colour, the houses and shops reflected the grandeur of the Noble estate. "He loves history. Did I mention that he teaches the subject in Keterton?"

"Perhaps, once you have your home sorted, he might like to come see them," Sarah grinned. "We have records dating back to the birth of the estate."

"Oh, is that an orchard?" Laura asked, completely lost in the beauty of the past now. "And look at those fields! The whole area was magnificent. Not that it isn't lovely, now. I just never expected to see the comparison to our modern day.

And there is the cottage again. I still don't see any clues that might lead us to the answers but look how darling it is with the garden beside it. That is just what I hope to achieve next spring."

She studied the old books one at a time with her new friends. Each glimpse into the past made Laura long to restore Adington to its former glory. There were areas where she saw potential to surpass it, as well.

"You don't suppose there was once some sort of tunnel between the main house and the gamekeeper's cottage, do you?" She asked when the photographs began to take on colour. "Perhaps one would have been used to transport game to the kitchens?"

"I don't believe so," Jane shook her head. "I would have found it as a child if one ever existed. I was notorious for seeking out secret passages and exploring areas that I was expressly forbidden to enter. I was a bit of a tomboy in my youth. Let me see if I can find a picture."

"She forgets to say that she dragged me along on her explorations until I was old enough to have the good sense to say no," Sarah smoothed her skirt like the refined lady she was before giving her sister a twinkling smile. "I am sure we would have found a secret tunnel if there was one to find. Perhaps a coal Shute? That might explain the acrid smell, as well."

"We haven't found signs of one." Laura reached for the edge of the page and her hand froze. Ice water immediately fizzed through her veins and her heart lurched almost painfully. "Wait. When was this picture taken?"

"Oh, that's my Peter," Jane sighed. "This was taken before he knew he was mine, of course. I believe it would have been in the early spring of 1952. If memory serves me, it was right after he was hired as our gamekeeper. I remember looking over my father's shoulder and wondering what caused him to hire someone so young. Then, I took a good hard look at Peter Marsh, and I saw the reason as clear as day. His feet had barely had time to get used to the feel of our land and there he was standing on it like he had grown from the soil itself. I believe I may have fallen in love with him that instant although it took me until mid-summer to admit as much to myself. Peter was chasing the wrong girl at the time. I couldn't allow that. In hindsight, I was a bit impetuous about the whole affair."

"You can't blame yourself, Jane," Sarah laid her hand on Jane's shoulder soothingly. "We were all so young. No one saw the consequences to come while we were in the midst of it. Not even Sally. She was tattling because her feelings were hurt, and the old green-eyed monster got the better of her. Father, too. The whole horrible episode was driven by far too many unpleasant feelings."

Laura's mouth felt dry. The conversation between the sisters sounded distant and garbled behind the ringing in her ears. She couldn't tear her eyes away from the picture of Peter Marsh. His image stared back at her with the same pleasant smile she had chased along the river earlier. Two black labs, identical in every way to the pair loping along the water's edge, sat beside the long-dead gamekeeper in front of the cottage.

"Laura?" Jane reached across the table to touch the younger woman's hand. "What is it, dear? What has you so upset?"

"It's him," Laura whispered. "That's the man Jay and I saw swept away in the flood. It's the same man I couldn't catch up to this morning. I swear it is. The dogs, too. It can't be. I know that. They have all been gone since before I was born. I saw them, though. All of them. It was just this morning. How?"

"Perhaps it's some distant cousin?" Sarah said calmingly.

"Peter had no family," Jane clutched the locket

tighter. "It's why he came to the estate. The War took the last of them. He was far too young to fight in it and was sent to the countryside during the bombings in London. By the time it was over, he had no one left to go back to."

"A strange coincidence, then," Sarah assured them both.

"He's wearing the same hat," Laura wiped tears from her eyes as she choked on her description. "The same vest, too. I could accept a similarity of build or hair colour. Labrador retrievers are a popular breed. But the rest? Its him"

"I BELIEVE you and I should take a walk down to the river," Jane's eyes filled with tears, "He's come back for me"

In the face of Jane's determination, there was nothing Laura or Sarah could do, she had always been a free spirit and done exactly what she wanted. "Let's go," said Jane. "NOW shrieked Sarah. "Yes Sarah, now, before it's too late."

THE THREE OF them set out, there was a bench midway down that should give them a good view of the comings and goings. Sarah had brought a warm plaid blanket with her so at least Jane would have the added warmth of it. They got to the bench and the three of them sat, jane in the middle and the blanket over their knees.

"We are nearing the time when the Autumn Festival took place, it is an anniversary of sorts. A dark one in this case, as it is when Peter was killed. He will have come back to find me, but instead he found you and Jay in his house. I am so sorry Laura that he has frightened you both, he would never have done that. He must be so confused; he was such a gentle loving soul, he has waited a long time for me, he comes back every year to see if I am ready to join him"

"You have seen him then Jane" Laura was stunned. "Oh yes, many many times, at the cottage and at the river, that's why I kept the cottage to myself for so long. But its time Laura, I am ready to go home, to be in his arms again. That's why I sold the cottage, but I didn't think the timing through and of course you had already moved in before the anniversary of his death during the "Autumn Festival" which is this week. Sarah put her hand on Janes and the ladies sat together as if their thoughts were blending in a silent knowing. "He is early this year"

Sarah said, "Jane smiled "he knows I am ready Sarah" and the sisters squeezed each other's hands.

Tell us your plans for the cottage Laura, I am excited to hear what you and Jay are going to do. The old place is crying out for new life, after been held back in time for so long.

"I HAVE such plans for it, Jane, and now that I have seen those old pictures, ideas are buzzing through me for Adington, too. Bringing back the orchard and nurturing the gardens back into their floral glory. I am going to build a green house and grow herbs and encourage wild flowers. We will clear the footpaths to the river again and care for the forest" Jane and Sarah nodded and smiled.

When the silence stretched out, Jane turned a quizzical eye to Laura.

"What about bringing back the Autumn Festival?" Laura bit her bottom lip. Well we had discussed that when Martin at the pub talked about it, but now I know what happened I wouldn't want to upset you.

"I always loved the festival," Jane's eyes softened. "I was never very good at sticking to the jobs I was given, but I did love how the village all came together to celebrate the turning of the season. When I was a child, there were so many parties throughout the year. Our mother orchestrated most of them. After she passed, Father threw himself into the business side when it came to most of the entertainment that the estate hosted. That, and raising his daughters. There wasn't time for the rest. He kept the Autumn Festival alive because it was the last chance the village had to have a bit of fun before winter set in. After what happened, no one's heart was in it any longer. It is past time that changed. One grief-stricken day should not haunt those who are far too young to be punished by it, don't you think?"

"I do," Laura caught a stray tear at the corner of her eye on a knuckle and smiled sadly. "It's odd to say, but I can feel the sadness here sometimes. Especially at the cottage and now sitting beside you. It's like there is a blanket of it over the village that everyone here has gotten used to. Most ignore it if they feel it at all. Maybe bringing some of the joy back would throw it off entirely."

"I will write a note to make sure my mother's planning books make it into your hands. They are doing no one any good sitting in a dusty trunk in the attic. You could see if they hold any useful ideas. I was very young when she died but I do remember her having a bountifully creative spirit," Jane turned to Sarah "What do you think?" "Oh yes it will be wonderful, I will dig them out and you can have them Laura." Them Jane turned her head and fell silent. Her breath caught with a gasp and her old heart gave a mighty thump. She reached out to clutch Laura's hand in an iron grip. "It's him."

Laura was on her feet, scanning the riverwalk before Jane and Sarah could push themselves up from the bench. Sure enough, the man they had been waiting to see was walking toward them at the edge of the water. His dogs trotted beside him eagerly.

"Peter?" His name escaped Jane's lips in a breathless whisper.

The man raised his arm in a wave. This was the closest Laura had ever been to him. His resemblance to Peter Marsh from the photographs was even more uncanny now that she saw his face so clearly.

Jane's hand shook as she raised it to the locket hanging over her heart. Impossible or not, she was sure of what she saw. Not time, nor death itself, could change the truth. Peter Marsh was walking toward her, love shining in his twinkling eyes. He stopped some distance away and squatted down to talk to the dogs. Duke and Squire immediately turned toward Jane, romping over as they had so many years ago. The beautiful pain of the moment wove itself around her until tears of utter joy welled in her faded eyes.

Peter stood once more and cocked his head as he always did when he saw her coming. His hands settled on his hips with mock annoyance. Then, his smile blossomed on those perfect lips that had once kissed her so passionately. He held out his hand as if beckoning her. He shook his Then, he set out to close the distance between them.

"It's Peter, Laura. It's my Peter. I don't care how or why," Jane squeezed Laura's hand. "I just know it's him." Jane began to walk toward him as steady and sure footed as a woman half her age. Jane took Laura's hand and said quietly "let her go" so they sat and watched her walk towards him. As they reached each other they became hazy as if fog had rolled across their path. Then, just as quickly as they Peter and his dog's had appeared, they vanished.

Jane turned and walked back towards them, there was no fear in her, no tears, either. Too much joy filled her. Wonder pushed out any sense of disquiet that might have tried to take root when she first saw him standing there with his trusty dogs at his side. Laura raced to her side.

"I'm glad I insisted on coming," she said softly. "More than glad. Thank you, Laura. We can go home now. As for the cottage, I have a feeling your troubles are at an end. I can feel it as surely as I can tell you that my love is just here to collect me. I believe he may have gotten a bit confused while he was waiting. I suppose that may be excusable under the circumstances. Please don't think too badly of him."

Laura's legs felt rubbery, and her mouth was too dry to say anything even if there were words for what she had just witnessed. Part of her brain was still spinning on itself trying to come up with some logical explanation. Her heart knew that the only one to be found was in Jane's smile.

They made it back to the house Jane shared with Sarah without incident. Laura called Jay and asked him to join them once he left school for the day. She gave him no further details. Those could wait until he arrived. Maybe by then, she would stop feeling as if the world she knew had been turned on its head. The rules for reality that she had woken with this morning were gone. They evaporated right along with Peter Marsh and his dogs. She wondered if Jay would be able to believe any of it. She laughed to herself. History was filled with ghost stories. He might take this one in his stride and breathe a sigh of relief that his troubles were due to nothing more than a restless spirit confused about where he should focus his search for love.

"Oh good, you are getting some of your colour back," Sarah filled Laura's cup with a fresh brew of chamomile tea and added a second delicate cake to the plate in front of her. "I was beginning to worry."

"Today has been nothing at all like what I thought it was meant to be when I got out of bed," Laura laughed. "I'm still not sure what to do with it. How is Jane?"

"She is resting," Sarah's eyes took on a gentle sadness. "She told me everything while I helped her to bed. I know it sounds unreasonable, but I can't help but believe her. Maybe I am even a bit hopeful that my Richard will come back for me one day. My sister's heart has been broken for so long that I fear it may give out now that it has been put back together. I have accepted that, too. She refuses to let me call the doctor. I suppose that is her right, although I will be dreadfully lonely if she decides to let Peter collect her. At eighty-seven, it hardly seems fair to insist that she wait until I'm ready to go as well."

"You don't believe that she could, 'will' herself to die, do you?" Laura asked horrified. This was not at all what she wanted. Jane Noble's age might be advanced but that was no reason to give up on whatever time she might have left. "Jane is such a strong woman. So filled with life. Surely, she will be fine after a bit of sleep."

"She has been ill since June," Sarah sighed. "The doctor told us that she might not see another winter. Jane was relieved by the news. She has her own way of looking at life. Leaving it behind was never something that worried her. She always laughed and said that she was the last person to argue the natural order of things."

"Should I stay? I could be the one to call the doctor so you wouldn't be going against her wishes. I feel that this is all my fault. I never meant to -" Laura began.

"Never meant to bring Jane the peace that she has searched for most of her life?" Sarah shook her head. "Don't be silly, Laura. You have done nothing wrong. You should go home when your husband arrives. You need to make sure that the cottage is at peace, too. I agree with my sister on that as well. Now that Peter knows that he doesn't have to watch over his old home and that his love is on her way, I think you will find the cottage is warm and cozy once more."

"I think so, too," Laura wondered if it would feel empty when they went inside, too. Even with all the strangeness, the thought stirred an echo of sadness within her. "I don't care if that should sound foolish or not. I can feel the change in the air. I know that Jane and I saw Peter's spirit. My heart knows what that means even if my brain doesn't want to believe any of it."

There was a knock at the door.

"That will be Jay," Laura got up on legs that were much stronger than the ones she walked in with. "If you are sure that you don't want me to stay, I will slip out, so we don't disturb you any further."

"Only if you promise to come back and visit," Sarah took Laura's hand in both of hers. "I can't put into words what your coming here has done for us. Please know that it was all good. I don't want any nonsense seeping in and telling you otherwise. I am looking forward to meeting your Jay and convincing him to help me with a bit of a winter project. I think it's time for Adington's story to be told the right way."

"We will come back," Laura assured her. Then, she looked toward the stairs where Jane had gone almost as soon as they returned. "Give Jane my love. Tell her...Just tell her that I wish her nothing but happiness and that I am grateful for the chance to get to know her."

"Is everything alright, Laura?" Jay asked when his wife slipped out the door of the house he had been told to meet her at. "I thought you wanted to show me something."

"Another day," Laura wrapped her arms around him and breathed him in deeply. "There are some things we need to check on first. Then, I need to tell you a most remarkable story. I swear every word of it is true, so you have to promise to believe me no matter how strange it sounds. Can you do that?"

When he agreed with a bemused grin, she wrapped her arm through his and led the way to the pub knowing it would all go down far better with food in their bellies and a pint or two to help it settle. No matter how hard Laura looked, she saw no trace of Peter Marsh or the two dogs.

For the first time, Harvey trotted happily beside them as they went to the cottage. The door was closed firmly when they arrived. No hint of gunpowder lingered in the air. When Jay turned the fuses on, the lights shone bright and steady.

"It feels different," Jay declared after walking

from room to room. "It's still a mess, mind you, but something has changed."

"It feels calm," Laura sighed. "Peaceful, even, and warm!"

"I would have never thought to blame a draft on the ghost of the former occupant," Jay chuckled. "Had I known that was the cause of it all, I would have offered him a beer and we could have sorted it all out like men. Do you think I reminded him of John Noble in some way? Is that why he kept hiding my tools from me?"

"Possibly," Laura shrugged. Jay took the whole tale in stride and accepted it far more easily than she had. She shouldn't have been surprised. He lived and worked with spirits of the past every day. Finding one in his new home didn't come as quite the shock it might have to someone less involved with the past. "And maybe I reminded him just a tiny bit of Jane when she was younger. I saw photos of her and there are similarities even if they are small."

"So much tragedy," Jay sighed. "It's a wonder anyone from that time stuck around. Villages have fallen into ruin for less."

"It says a lot about our new neighbours, I think."

Laura breathed in the peace of her new home. If she closed her eyes, she could look past the current mess and see the beauty that awaited them. "I'm glad we came here, Jay."

"Me too," he wrapped an arm around her and snuggled her close. "But I suggest we wait until tomorrow to start putting this place back together. I think we've had enough excitement for one day."

Word came at breakfast. Jane Noble had passed peacefully in her sleep the night before. Sarah found her smiling as if still caught in a pleasant dream when she took her breakfast up.

"I guess I knew when I left the house yesterday," Laura said wistfully. "I do wish you could have met her, though. She was such a lovely woman."

"Jane is back with her love," Jay assured her as he unlocked the cottage door. "It seems like the best ending anyone can hope for.''

As if to make sure Laura knew that to be true, she found the shattered tiles in the bathtub made a hole again. This time, they were fused into a solid heart with barely a crack visible. Laura called to Jay through happy tears, and she put the heart away until the spring when Laura planned to put it on display. She just needed to decide if it would find its home in the clearing where Duke and Squire rested or at the cottage where Jane and Peter's love grew so strong that death itself couldn't tear them apart.

EPILOGUE

As winter set in, Adington somehow grew cozier. Decades under the sombre cloud that descended the day Peter Marsh died disappeared overnight. The villagers joked about it out loud while at the same time, many took up the old tradition of sweeping the fog back out the door in the mornings.

Laura made it a habit of visiting with Sarah often. It was one of the highlights of her busy week. Now that the cottage was whole again, Laura could finally turn her focus to the future.

Jay was busy, too. He and Sarah were writing a book about the Noble estate and its village. They both agreed that the past made Adington what it was today and preserving it for future generations was a worthy goal. Their book was meant to bring history back to life, and they were well on their way to doing just that already. Every evening was spent at the dining room table making sure that they got it right while Laura made sketches from the old photographs and took notes from Sarah's mother's journal. Harvey claimed a spot in the corner where he dozed contentedly unless Sarah lured him away with some ham.

They were happy days even when the winds that carried ice and snow blanketed the riverwalk. Adington became Jay and Laura's home as much as the cottage where the seeds of their dream took shape.

Now and again, Laura felt someone watching over her shoulder as she worked. Warmth would pass through her as if her efforts were approved. Harvey would perk up for a moment and wag his tail. Sometimes, he would roll his ball across the floor and watch to see if it might be returned. Although it never was, the little terrier never gave up hope. Jay nearly always found some new information that was exactly what he needed for the book in those moments. He would smile and whisper his thanks for the help he received. Then, his pen would begin scratching across the paper once more with renewed vigour.

SARAH SOMETIMES FELT the strong presence of her sister. "Jane," she would say, and would close her eyes and smile every time it happened. The moments passed quickly and were few and far between, but they were treasured all the more for it. "Go on now. You've got far better things to do than hover here. I'll be along one of these days' sweet sister but until then, if you see Richard tell him that all is well. The family we created would make him proud.

OVER A YEAR HAD PASSED since Laura and Jay had moved to Keeper's Cottage, and for the first time since 1954, the Adington Village Autumn Festival was well under way. Sarah had helped with the planning and was guest of Honour.

The crisp autumn air carried the scent of spiced cider and roasted chestnuts as Laura and Jay's village festival came to life in the field in front of the village inn that was formerly the family home of the Noble family, the local landowners during the 1900s. It was a celebration of harvest and heritage. Strings of golden fairy lights twinkled between stalls brimming with homemade jams, hand-knitted scarves, and artisan crafts, while the aroma of fresh-baked potatoes and sizzling sausages filled the air. Children laughed as they bobbed for apples and painted pumpkins, while a lively folk band played traditional tunes near the old oak tree. The guest of honour, Sarah, who's Father, John Noble had started the village festival in 1945, beamed as she cut the ribbon to open the event, her memories woven into every tradition revived. Nearby, the tug-of-war contest gathered eager competitors, and the hay bale maze echoed with excited giggles. As dusk fell, lanterns were lit, and the evening concluded with a storytelling session by the bonfire, where Sarah shared tales of past festivals, bridging the past with the present in the heart of the village she loved.

As Jay and Laura lay in their bed in Keepers Cottage that night, exhausted and happy after a successful festival, they felt blessed that the trauma of the early months in the cottage was over and life had settled into the best it possibly could be. They were so happy here, they had made new friends and their old friends loved to visit. Business had taken off for Laura and she was loving her new way of working. Jay had been made head of History at his school and was enjoying the more relaxed environment of a rural school compared to the city. "Do you think Peter and Jane were at the festival today Jay?" Jay could tell Laura was smiling as she spoke even though it was dark. "Of course they were and probably Sarah's husband Richard too. I think they would all be very proud." Yes, I think so too" Laura sighed "I wonder if John Noble really did kill Peter, or if it was an accident? We have read so much about him whilst doing this book research and he comes across as a kind family man, it's hard to believe he could have done that, don't you think?". "I don't know Laura, people can be pushed into doing crazy things if the circumstances align."

"Night my beautiful clever wife" Jay hugged her close, and she was already asleep.

Jay stirred in his sleep, a suffocating chill wrapping around him like a damp shroud. A whisper, low and rasping, breathed his name. His eyes snapped open, and his blood ran cold. A figure loomed over the bed, with a face pale and skeletal, eyes black hollows that burned into him. The stench of gun powder filled the room. Jay's throat locked, but then a scream tore from him, raw and desperate. The figure didn't move, didn't blink, just stared. "Christ,

Laura! It's him... it's *John Noble!*" He sat bolt upright and scrambled away from the figure so his back was against the headboard, his heart hammering against his ribs. Laura jerked awake as Jay's panic sent tremors through the bed. She reached for him, but he was rigid, his wide eyes fixed on the empty space where, just moments ago, John Noble had risen from the dead.

END

ALSO BY CHARLOTTE WEBB

The Haunting of Holly House

The Haunting of Holly House

Meadowbank School for Girls is steeped in history, tradition, and whispers of a dark past.

As the Christmas term draws to a close, excitement buzzes through the boarding house—plays to write, parties to attend, and secrets lurking beneath the surface.

For Lizzy, Rosie, Emma and Dawn the task is simple: choose a prop, create a 20-minute play, and perform it before the school. But when they uncover a dusty Ouija board hidden beneath the stage, their innocent production turns into something far more sinister.

As they dabble with the supernatural, the line between make-believe and reality blurs.

Mysterious messages begin to emerge from the board, eerily connected to Holly House's dark past. Icy chills, unexplainable shadows, and terrifying encounters shake the girls' sense of safety. Strange occurrences aren't just coincidence—something malevolent has awakened.

Flashbacks to 1875 reveal a twisted love affair, a scorned housemistress, and a groundskeeper's dangerous obsession. And as Lizzy unravels the haunting story, she realizes the ghost isn't a stranger at all—it's bound to her by secrets of the past.

In *"The Haunting Of Holly House"* secrets refuse to stay buried, and spirits won't rest until their story is told.

Gripping, atmospheric, and spine-chilling, this supernatural thriller will leave you questioning how far the past can reach into the present—and what happens when it refuses to let go.

Are you ready to discover who—or what—is pushing the glass?

The Lighthouse

The Lighthouse - A Ghost Story

The lighthouse cottage stands on a windswept cliff, surrounded by breathtaking views of sea and sky—a place where time seems to stand still. Its beauty feels almost otherworldly, a tranquil haven far removed from the chaos of modern life. But beneath its serene surface lies something far darker, an unseen force rooted in the cottage's tragic past.

For Emily, the new resident, the ghosts of the past are not just echoes or fleeting memories. They begin as whispers on the wind, cold spots in the cozy cottage, and flickering lights in the dead of night. At first, the disturbances seem harmless, even explainable. But as the weeks pass, they become more invasive, slipping into her dreams and, eventually, her waking life. When the hauntings turn physical, Emily realises the spirits are not just restless—they're angry.

Sometimes, the ghosts of the past refuse to let go.

The Water Mill

<u>The Mill House</u>

When the Harper family moves to a remote, abandoned water mill in Anglesey, North Wales, they dream of a fresh start.

The secluded beauty of the old mill promises to be an inspiration for artists Steve and Abi's paintings and sculptures and a perfect setting for the gallery they plan to open. They long for a peaceful life away from the chaos of the city.

But the mill holds more than just history within its walls,

it harbours secrets, shadows, and something that refuses to rest.

As the past injustice and the desire for revenge seeps into the present, it threatens to destroy the Harpers lives.

They are drawn into a dark mystery that will test their courage and their relationship. The millpond's hidden secrets are told by unseen voices, the shadows shift, and the darkness begins to rise.

ABOUT THE AUTHOR

You are warmly invited to download Charlotte's first, free little book, and to connect with her on Facebook.

Here you can keep up to date with new releases and join in to chat about everything spooky and paranormal.

Ravencross Road (Download for free)

Facebook Page (Please like and follow)

Facebook Group - Charlotte's Haunted House

Charlotte Webb is a gifted author with a passion for all things paranormal. Her love for ghosts and the supernatural led her to run a business in the UK, taking curious thrill-seekers to haunted locations steeped in mystery. With firsthand experiences in some of the country's most eerie sites, Charlotte brings a vivid authenticity to her writing, drawing readers into chilling tales that feel all too real. Her books weave fact and fiction seamlessly, blending her encounters with an imagination that knows no bounds, offering readers a window into the worlds where shadows move, secrets linger, and the past never truly fades away.

Charlotte now resides in an old cottage in a small Northamptonshire village which is steeped in history and holds many ghost stories of its own. She shares her home with her husband, five rescue dogs, four parrots, and a lively flock of chickens and ducks. One of her books is set in this very home, and tells the story of a true ghostly character that has been seen many times in the countryside around her cottage.

Can you tell which is fact or fiction?

Printed in Great Britain
by Amazon